100
Greatest
Love Letters

Terry O'Brien is a bestselling author of several books, an academician, a freelance broadcaster, a quiz enthusiast and a motivational trainer. He is a man of many parts, a language expert, a connoisseur of literature, a versatile writer on a plethora of subjects and a trainer's trainer.

100 Greatest Love Letters

Selected and Edited by
TERRY O'BRIEN

Published by
Rupa Publications India Pvt. Ltd 2024
7/16, Ansari Road, Daryaganj
New Delhi 110002

Sales centres:
Bengaluru Chennai
Hyderabad Jaipur Kathmandu
Kolkata Mumbai Prayagraj

Edition copyright © Rupa Publications India Pvt. Ltd 2024
Selection and Introduction copyright © Terry O'Brien 2024

All rights reserved.
No part of this publication may be reproduced, transmitted,
or stored in a retrieval system, in any form or by any means,
electronic, mechanical, photocopying, recording or otherwise,
without the prior permission of the publisher.

P-ISBN: 978-93-90260-50-8
E-ISBN: 978-93-90260-90-4

Third impression 2024

10 9 8 7 6 5 4 3

Printed in India

This book is sold subject to the condition that it shall not,
by way of trade or otherwise, be lent, resold, hired out, or otherwise
circulated, without the publisher's prior consent, in any form of
binding or cover other than that in which it is published.

Contents

Introduction ix

1. John Keats to Fanny Brawne 1
2. Beethoven to Unnamed 'Immortal Beloved' 4
3. Honoré de Balzac to Evelina Hańska 8
4. Mozart to Constanze Weber 10
5. Voltaire to Olympe Dunover 12
6. Lewis Carroll to May Mileham, Adelaide Paine and Gertrude Chataway 14
7. Leo Tolstoy to Valeria Arsenev 19
8. Robert Browning to Elizabeth Barrett Browning 20
9. Zelda Fitzgerald to F. Scott Fitzgerald 24
10. William Congreve to Arabella Hunt 27
11. Oscar Wilde to Lord Alfred 'Bosie' Douglas 29
12. Emma Darwin to Charles Darwin 34
13. Napoleon Bonaparte to Joséphine de Beauharnais 36
14. Sir Walter Raleigh to Elizabeth Raleigh 41
15. Lord Byron to Teresa Guiccioli 45
16. Henry VIII to Anne Boleyn 47
17. Benjamin Franklin to Anne Brillon 50
18. Robert Burns to Agnes Maclehose 52
19. Nathaniel Hawthorne to Sophia Peabody 55
20. George Bernard Shaw to Beatrice Campbell 59

21.	Pliny the Younger to Calpurnia	60
22.	Marilyn Monroe to Joe DiMaggio	61
23.	Richard Steele to Mary Scurlock	62
24.	James Joyce to Nora Barnacle	64
25.	Dylan Thomas to Caitlin Thomas	66
26.	Alexander Pope to Martha Blount	68
27.	Eleanor Roosevelt to Lorena Hickok	71
28.	Vita Sackville-West to Virginia Woolf	72
29.	Lord Byron to Lady Caroline Lamb	74
30.	Victor Hugo to Adele Foucher	76
31.	Alfred de Musset to George Sand	79
32.	Robert Schumann to Clara Wieck	80
33.	Gustave Flaubert to Louise Colet	83
34.	Mark Twain to Olivia Langdon	84
35.	Pierre Curie to Marie Curie	86
36.	G.K. Chesterton to Frances Blogg	88
37.	Allen Ginsberg to Peter Orlovsky	89
38.	Michael Faraday to Sarah Barnard	92
39.	Jean-Paul Sartre to Simone de Beauvoir	94
40.	Thomas Otway to Elizabeth Barry	97
41.	Winston Churchill to Clementine Churchill	99
42.	Juliette Drouet to Victor Hugo	101
43.	Edgar Allan Poe to Annie L. Richmond	103
44.	George Washington to Sarah Cary Fairfax	107
45.	Mary Wollstonecraft to William Godwin	110
46.	Isadora Duncan to Gordon Craig	112
47.	Tsarina Alexandra to Tsar Nicholas II of Russia	114

48.	Charlie Parker to Chan Parker	116
49.	Radclyffe Hall to Evguenia Souline	117
50.	Violet Trefusis to Vita Sackville-West	119
51.	Love Letters in William Shakespeare's Plays	121
52.	Esther Vanhomrigh to Jonathan Swift	124
53.	Abigail Adams to John Adams	126
54.	Emily Dickinson to Susan Gilbert	129
55.	Leigh Hunt to Marianne Kent Hunt	131
56.	Mary Hutchinson Wordsworth to William Wordsworth	133
57.	Claire Clairmont to Lord Byron	135
58.	John Ruskin to Effie Gray	137
59.	Edith Wharton to W. Morton Fullerton	138
60.	Sullivan Ballou to Sarah Ballou	141
61.	Warren G. Harding to Carrie Fulton Phillips	145
62.	Pietro Bembo to Lucrezia Borgia	146
63.	Elizabeth Barrett Browning to Robert Browning	148
64.	Prince Albert to Queen Victoria	151
65.	Charlotte Brontë to Professor Constantin Héger	153
66.	Catherine of Aragon to Henry VIII	154
67.	Henry IV of France to Gabrielle d'Estrées	156
68.	Ernest Hemingway to Marlene Dietrich	158
69.	Vincent van Gogh to Theo van Gogh (About His Cousin 'Kee')	161
70.	Heinrich von Kleist to Adolfine Henriette Vogel	162
71.	Oliver Cromwell to Elizabeth Cromwell	163
72.	Jane Baillie Welsh to Thomas Carlyle	165
73.	Jack London to Anna Strunsky	166

74.	Woodrow Wilson to Edith Galt Wilson	167
75.	Dorothy Osborne to Sir William Temple	169
76.	Harriet Beecher Stowe to Calvin Ellis Stowe	173
77.	Herman Melville to Nathaniel Hawthorne	176
78.	Mary Wollstonecraft to Gilbert Imlay	178
79.	Captain Frederick Wentworth to Anne Elliot	181
80.	Love Letters in Thomas Hardy's Poetry	183
81.	Franz Liszt to Marie D'Agoult	185
82.	Charles Dickens to Maria Beadnell	187
83.	Love Letters in William Butler Yeats' Poetry	189
84.	Anne Boleyn to Henry VIII	190
85.	John Rodgers to Minerva Denison	194
86.	Love Letters in Dante Gabriel Rossetti's Poetry	197
87.	Love Letters in Robert Herrick's Poetry	198
88.	Love Letters in Ben Jonson's Poetry	201
89.	Katherine Mansfield to John Middleton Murry	203
90.	Love Letters in Richard Lovelace's Poetry	206
91.	Subhas Chandra Bose to Emilie Schenkl	208
92.	Rupert Brooke to Noël Olivier	210
93.	Margery Paston to John Paston	212
94.	David Hume to Madame de Boufflers	215
95.	Count Gabriel Honoré de Mirabeau to Marie Thérèse de Monnier (Sophie)	217
96.	Robert Peary to Josephine Peary	219
97.	Julia Lee-Booker to Lieutenant Pat McSwiney	221
98.	Virginia Woolf to Vita Sackville-West	222
99.	Karl Marx to Jenny Von Westphalen	223
100.	Fyodor Dostoevsky to Anna Dostoevskaya	226

Introduction

The times today are mostly made up of brief moments of instant gratification, instant coffee and instant noodles; online romance that vanishes at the flicker of a computer screen.

Writing began with a quill, gradually moving to the fountain pen, thereafter to the ballpoint pen and finally to computers. There were times when love letters were treasured like birthday cards, Christmas cards and New Year cards. They seemed to be like a rose pressed among the yellow leaves of a book that has never been opened. Today's world is of the SMS: the shorter the message, the better it seems. It may contain passionate momentary messages, or it may also be just an emoticon! With *hallyu* or the Korean wave today; the sign of love is no longer just a heart…it is now **finger hearts**, also called Korean Finger Hearts, because they are associated with the rise of South Korean pop culture. The SMS parlance is laziness personified. In a flash, the message vanishes and so does the passion of a person: so there is no better moment than now to read those passionate letters that have passed the test of time.

Please do not let your emotions flicker away in a flash of light. A real love letter is made of insight, understanding, passion, compassion and even the occasional oddity; otherwise, it's not a love letter.

Dylan Thomas once wrote: 'I love you more than anybody in the world… I love you for millions and millions of things, clocks and vampires and dirty nails and squiggly paintings and lovely hair and being...'

Katherine Mansfield spelt it differently: 'You might drop your heart into me and you'd never hear it touch bottom.'

Johnny Cash, the singer, wrote: 'The fire and excitement may be gone now that we don't go out there and sing them anymore, but the ring of fire still burns around you and I, keeping our love hotter than a pepper sprout.'

Georgia O'Keeffe said: 'Dearest—my body is simply crazy with wanting you... I wonder if your body wants mine the way mine wants yours—the kisses—the hotness—the wetness—all melting together.'

In a letter to Fanny Brawne, Keats once wrote: 'My love is selfish. I cannot breathe without you.' Further he wrote: 'Love is my religion. I could die for it. I could die for you.'

It may go beyond just the bodily: 'The tragedy of sexual intercourse is the perpetual virginity of the soul,' said W.B. Yeats, who was in a relationship with Maud Gonne.

Here we present such timeless letters that can move mountains and still remain shining in the galaxy of timeless poetry that emerges from the fountain of love.

When two lovers meet, they often communicate with their eyes, and while they look at each other, words fail to reveal all the passion within them. But when they take to writing a love letter, they pour out all their feelings, embodying the expression: 'My great religion is a belief in the blood [...] We can go wrong in our minds. But what our blood feels and believes and says, is always true.' John Keats once wrote about his poetry something which may also be an adage for his love letters: 'The occasional intoxication of the blood.'

The inspiratus of a kiss could change one's life in a flash—

Alas how easily things go wrong!
A sigh too much, a kiss too long,
And there follows a mist and a weeping rain
And life is never the same again.

Love is not just temporal or transient; Robert Browning in a poem wrote: 'Leave now for dogs and apes! Man has forever.'

'I don't ask you to love me always like this, but I ask you to remember. Somewhere inside me there'll always be the person I am tonight,' said F. Scott Fitzgerald.

It's no surprise that Keats, in his short life of 25 years, desired to have just three years of butterflies in a warm summer with Fanny Brawne rather than 50 years of life!

Rousseau describes the poetics of writing a love letter: 'To write a good love letter, you ought to begin without knowing what you mean to say, and to finish without knowing what you have written.' Authenticity and sincerity are the capstone of this art.

Perhaps men who write love letters par excellence don't live in the present tense. So here comes a book up for grabs to celebrate Cupid's missive. This book cannot be completely written until someone else has read it: now it's your turn.

Yours affectionately,
Terry O'Brien

Kindly note:
(a) The love letters have been selected randomly and are not in chronological order.
(b) Some of the letters contained in this book are excerpts from longer letters.

1

John Keats to Fanny Brawne

John Keats was an English romantic poet of the nineteenth century who met Fanny Brawne in November 1818 in London, where he was staying at his friend's place. When Keats's brother Tom died of tuberculosis, Fanny proved to be a loving and supportive friend, which led to Keats falling in love with her. Keats died of tuberculosis at the young age of 25. As a romantic poet, his creativity was psychosomatic: the body affected the mind. His preoccupation with the theme of death is found in his poems:

> I have been half in love with easeful Death,
> Call'd him soft names in many a mused rhyme,
> To take into the air my quiet breath.

But Keats the man was one who believed in aesthetics and beauty. He once wrote, 'A thing of beauty is a joy for ever.' In fact, he further wrote: 'Beauty is truth, truth beauty.' Thus, his love for his beloved shows a unique side of him and his old love letters are fondly remembered. They embody his belief: 'Axioms of philosophy are no axioms unless they are felt upon the pulses.'

(13 October 1819)

My dearest Girl,

This moment I have set myself to copy some verses out fair. I cannot proceed with any degree of content. I must write you a line or two and see if that will assist in dismissing you from my Mind for ever so short a time. Upon my Soul I can think of nothing else—The time is passed when I had power to advise and warn you against the unpromising morning of my Life—My love has made me selfish. I cannot exist without you—I am forgetful of everything but seeing you again—my Life seems to stop there—I see no further. You have absorb'd me. I have a sensation at the present moment as though I was dissolving—I should be exquisitely miserable without the hope of soon seeing you. I should be afraid to separate myself far from you. My sweet Fanny, will your heart never change? My love, will it? I have no limit now to my love—Your note came in just here—I cannot be happier away from you—'T is richer than an Argosy of Pearles. Do not threat me even in jest. I have been astonished that Men could die Martyrs for religion—I have shudder'd at it—I shudder no more. I could be martyr'd for my Religion—Love is my religion—I could die for that—I could die for you. My Creed is Love and you are its only tenet—You have ravish'd me away by a Power I cannot resist; and yet I could resist till I saw you; and even since I have seen you I have endeavoured often 'to reason against the reasons of my Love.' I can do that no more—the pain would be too great—My Love is selfish. I cannot breathe without you.

Yours for ever
John Keats

(c. February 1820)

My sweet love,

I shall wait patiently till tomorrow before I see you, and in the mean time, if there is any need of such a thing, assure you by your Beauty, that whenever I have at any time written on a certain unpleasant subject, it has been with your welfare impress'd upon my mind. How hurt I should have been had you ever acceded to what is, notwithstanding, very reasonable! How much the more do I love you from the general result! In my present state of Health I feel too much separated from you and could almost speak to you in the words of Lorenzo's Ghost to Isabella

> 'Your Beauty grows upon me and I feel
> A greater love through all my essence steal.'

My greatest torment since I have known you has been the fear of you being a little inclined to the Cressid; but that suspicion I dismiss utterly and remain happy in the surety of your Love, which I assure you is as much a wonder to me as a delight. Send me the words 'Good night' to put under my pillow.

Dearest Fanny,
Your affectionate
J.K.

Old love letters are best remembered

2

Beethoven to Unnamed 'Immortal Beloved'

Ludwig van Beethoven was a German pianist and a composer. He is called the 'Father of the Romantic Era.' He wrote love letters addressed to a mysterious 'immortal beloved.' His letters were found after his death in March 1827. A lot of speculation surrounded the identity of this mysterious woman, but to date, nobody knows who the lady was.

The greatness of Beethoven was in the creativity of his music, despite his deafness. His dying words are memorable because of his faith in afterlife. He was deaf but his last words in life were: 'And I shall hear again in heaven.'

He once wrote, 'O do continue to love me—never misjudge your lover's most faithful heart.' His typical signature of love was spelt out:

> *Ever thine,*
> *Ever mine,*
> *Ever ours.*

(6 July, in the morning)

My angel, my all, my very self—Only a few words today, and, what is more, written in pencil (and with your pencil)—I shan't be certain of my rooms here until tomorrow; what an unnecessary waste of time is all this—Why this profound sorrow, when necessity speaks—can our love endure without sacrifices, without our demanding everything from one another, can you alter the fact that you are not wholly mine, that I am not wholly yours?—Dear God, look at Nature in all her beauty and set your heart at rest about what must be— Love demands all, and rightly so, and thus it is for me with you, for you with me—but you forget so easily that I must live for me and for you; if we were completely united, you would fee this painful necessity just as little as I do—My journey was dreadful and I did not arrive here until yesterday at four o'clock in the morning. As there were few horses the mail coach chose another route, but what a dreadful road it was; at the last state but one I was warned not to travel by night; attempts were made to frighten me about a forest, but all this only spurred me on to proceed—and it was wrong of me to do so. The coach broke down, of course, owing to the dreadful road which had not been made up and was nothing but a country track. If we hadn't had those two postillions I should have been left stranded on the way—On the other ordinary road Esterhazy with eight horses met with the same fate as I did with four— Yet I felt to a certain extent that pleasure I always feel when I have overcome some difficulty successfully—Well, let me turn quickly from outer to inner experiences. No doubt we shall meet soon; and today also time fails me to tell you of the thoughts which during these last few days I have been revolving about my life—If our hearts were always closely united, I would certainly entertain no such thoughts. My heart overflows with a longing to tell you so many things—Oh—there are moments when I find that speech is quite inadequate—Be cheerful—and be for ever my faithful, my only sweetheart, my all, as I am yours. The gods must send us everything else, whatever must and shall be our fate—

Your faithful Ludwig

(6 July, Monday evening)

You are suffering, you, my most precious one—I have noticed the very moment that letters have to be handed in very early, on Monday—or on Thursday—the only days when the mail coach goes from here to K[arlsbad].—You are suffering—Oh, where I am, you are with me—I will see to it that you and I, that I can live with you. What a life!!!! as it is now!!!! without you—pursued by the kindness of people here and there, a kindness that I think-that I wish to deserve just as little as I deserve it—man's homage to man—that pains me—and when I consider myself in the setting of the universe, what I am and what is the man—whom one calls the greatest of me—and yet—on the other hand therein lies the divine element in man—I weep when I think that probably you will not receive the first news of me until Saturday—However much you love me—good night—Since I am taking the baths I must get off to sleep—Dear God—so near! so far! Is not our love truly founded in heaven—and, what is more, as strongly cemented as the firmament of Heaven?—

(7 July, morning)

Even when I am in bed my thoughts rush to you, my eternally beloved, now and then joyfully, then again sadly, waiting to know whether Fate will hear our prayer—To face life I must live altogether with you or never see you. Yes, I am resolved to be a wanderer abroad until I can fly to your arms and say that I have found my true home with you and enfolded in your arms can let my soul be wafted to the realm on blessed spirits—alas, unfortunately it must be so—You will become composed, the more so as you know that I am faithful to you; no other woman can ever possess my heart—never—never— Oh God, why must one be separated from her who is so dear. Yet my life in V[ienna] at present is a miserable life—Your love has made me both the happiest and the unhappiest of mortals—At my age I now need stability and regularity in my life—can this coexist with our relationship?—Angel, I have just heard that the post goes every day—and therefore I must close, so that you may receive the letter immediately—Be calm; for only by calmly considering our lives can we achieve our purpose to live together—Be calm—love me—Today— yesterday—what tearful longing for you—for you—you—my life—my all—all good wishes to you—Oh, do continue to love me—never misjudge your lover's most faithful heart.
 ever yours
 ever mine
 ever ours

L.

Old love letters are best remembered

3

Honoré de Balzac to Evelina Hańska

Honoré de Balzac was an influential French writer famous for his masterpiece, La Comédie humaine *(The Human Comedy). In 1833, Balzac started writing to a young countess, Evelina Hańska, who Balzac fondly called 'Eva.' Both were in love with each other and wrote to each other for the next 17 years. Both married on 15 March 1850; but the marriage was short-lived, as Balzac passed away five months later.*

Balzac once wrote: 'True is eternal, infinite, and always…' He was beyond the judgemental: 'The more one judges, the less one loves.'

Balzac is regarded as one of the founders of realism in European literature.

⁂

(Sunday, 19 June 1836)

MY BELOVED ANGEL,

I am nearly mad about you, as much as one can be mad: I cannot bring together two ideas that you do not interpose yourself between them. I can no longer think of nothing but you. In spite of myself, my imagination carries me to you. I grasp you, I kiss you, I caress you, a thousand of the most amorous caresses take possession of me. As for my heart, there you will always be—very much so. I have a delicious sense of you there. But my God, what is to become of me, if you have deprived me of my reason? This is a monomania which, this morning, terrifies me. I rise up every moment say to myself, 'Come, I am going there!' Then I sit down again, moved by the sense of my obligations. There is a frightful conflict. This is not a life. I have never before been like that. You have devoured everything. I feel foolish and happy as soon as I let myself think of you. I whirl round in a delicious dream in which in one instant I live a thousand years. What a horrible situation! Overcome with love, feeling love in every pore, living only for love, and seeing oneself consumed by griefs, and caught in a thousand spiders' threads. O, my darling Eva, you did not know it. I picked up your card. It is there before me, and I talked to you as if you were here. I see you, as I did yesterday, beautiful, astonishingly beautiful. Yesterday, during the whole evening, I said to myself 'She is mine!' Ah! The angels are not as happy in Paradise as I was yesterday!

Old love letters are best remembered

4

Mozart to Constanze Weber

Wolfgang Amadeus Mozart, popularly called Mozart, was a prolific and influential composer of the classical period. Despite his short life, his rapid pace of composition resulted in more than 800 works across virtually every genre. Mozart is widely regarded as the greatest composer in the history of music. Significantly, he composed his first symphony at the early age of five—this indeed was a classic.

In 1781, Mozart fell in love with Constanze Weber, the sister of his old flame Aloysia. He was especially attracted to her singing. Constanze reciprocated his love and both married in 1782. He was a man of the heart. Thus, he wrote: 'I pay no attention whatever to anybody's praise or blame. I simply follow my own feelings.'

(30 September 1790)

Dearest little Wife of my heart!

If only I had a letter from you, everything would be all right.

[...]

Dearest, I have no doubt that I shall get something going here, but it won't be easy as you and some of our friends think.—It is true, I am known and respected here; but, well—No—let us just see what happens.—In any case, I do prefer to play it safe, that why I would like to conclude this deal with H…because I would get some money into my possession without having to pay any out; all I would have to do then is work, and I shall be only too happy to do that for my little wife.

[…]

I get all excited like a child when I think about being with you again—If people could see into my heart I should almost feel ashamed. Everything is cold to me—ice-cold.—If you were here with me, maybe I would find the courtesies people are showing me more enjoyable,—but as it is, it's all so empty—adieu—my dear—I am Forever

your Mozart who loves you
with his entire soul.

PS.—while I was writing the last page, tear after tear fell on the paper. But I must cheer up—catch—An astonishing number of kisses are flying about—The deuce!—I see a whole crowd of them. Ha! Ha!… I have just caught three—They are delicious… I kiss you millions of times.

Old love letters are best remembered

5

Voltaire to Olympe Dunover

François-Marie Arouet, popularly known as Voltaire, was a French writer, historian and philosopher. He was famous for his wit.

He fell in love with Olympe Dunover when he was the secretary to the French ambassador in Holland. But Voltaire's father disapproved of this and used a 'lettre de cachet' to have him imprisoned without trial so that both could not meet. Olympe could not take this and withdrew from the relationship. This left Voltaire heartbroken.

He stated, 'Love has features which pierce all hearts, he wears a bandage which conceals the faults of those beloved.' He once also said: 'Love is a canvas furnished by nature and embroidered by imagination.'

∫

(The Hague, 1713)

I am a prisoner here in the name of the King; they can take my life, but not the love that I feel for you. Yes, my adorable mistress, to-night I shall see you, and if I had to put my head on the block to do it.

For heaven's sake, do not speak to me in such disastrous terms as you write; you must live and be cautious; beware of madame your mother as of your worst enemy. What do I say? Beware of everybody; trust no one; keep yourself in readiness, as soon as the moon is visible; I shall leave the hotel incognito, take a carriage or a chaise, we shall drive like the wind to Sheveningen; I shall take paper and ink with me; we shall write our letters.

If you love me, reassure yourself; and call all your strength and presence of mind to your aid; do not let your mother notice anything, try to have your pictures, and be assured that the menace of the greatest tortures will not prevent me to serve you. No, nothing has the power to part me from you; our love is based upon virtue, and will last as long as our lives. Adieu, there is nothing that I will not brave for your sake; you deserve much more than that. Adieu, my dear heart!

Arout

Old love letters are best remembered

6

Lewis Carroll to May Mileham, Adelaide Paine and Gertrude Chataway

Charles Lutwidge Dodgson (pseudonym Lewis Carroll), famous for his Alice's Adventures in Wonderland, *was fond of children. He was an English author, poet and mathematician. He was noted for his facility with wordplay, logic and fantasy. Lewis Carroll was particularly affectionate towards little girls and this was thought as a way to deal with this loneliness because he did not marry.*

With a subtle ring of irony, he wrote: 'The one who loves the least, controls the relationship.'

To May Mileham

(7 Lushington Road, Eastbourne, 6 September 1885)

Dearest May,

Thank you very much indeed for the peaches. They were delicious. Eating one was almost as nice as kissing you; Of course not quite; I think, if I had to give the exact measurement, I should say three-quarters as nice; We are having such a lovely time here; and the sands are beautiful. I only wish I could some day come across you, washing your pocket-handkerchief in a pool among the rocks? But I wander on the beach, and look for you, in vain; and then I say, Where is May? And the stupid boatmen reply, 'It isn't May, sir? It's September?' But it doesn't comfort me.

Always your loving C.L.D.

To Adelaide Paine

(Christ Church, Oxford, 8 March 1880)

My dear Ada,—Isn't that your short name? 'Adelaide' is all very well, but you see when one's dreadfully busy one hasn't time to write such long words—particularly when it takes one half an hour to remember how to spell it—and even then one has to go and get a dictionary to see if one has spelt it right, and of course the dictionary is in another room, at the top of a high bookcase—where it has been for months and months, and has got all covered with dust—so one has to get a duster first of all, and nearly choke oneself in dusting it—and when one has made out at last which is dictionary and which is dust, even then there's the job of remembering which end of the alphabet 'A' comes—for one feels pretty certain it isn't in the middle—then one has to go and wash one's hands before turning over the leaves—for they've got so thick with dust one hardly knows them by sight—and, as likely as not, the soap is lost, and the jug is empty, and there's no towel, and one has to spend hours and hours in finding things—and perhaps after all one has to go off to the shop to buy a new cake of soap—

so, with all this bother, I hope you won't mind my writing it short and saying, 'My dear Ada'). You said in your last letter you would like a likeness of me: so here it is, and I hope you will like it—I won't forget to call the next time but one I'm in Wallington.

Your very affectionate friend,
Lewis Carroll.

To Gertrude Chataway

(Christ Church, Oxford, 13 October 1875)

My dear Gertrude,—I never give birthday presents, but you see I do sometimes write a birthday letter: so, as I've just arrived here, I am writing this to wish you many and many a happy return of your birthday to-morrow. I will drink your health, if only I can remember, and if you don't mind—but perhaps you object? You see, if I were to sit by you at breakfast, and to drink your tea, you wouldn't like that, would you? You would say 'Boo! hoo! Here's Mr. Dodgson's drunk all my tea, and I haven't got any left!' So I am very much afraid, next time Sybil looks for you, she'll find you sitting by the sad sea-wave, and crying 'Boo! hoo! Here's Mr. Dodgson has drunk my health, and I haven't got any left!' And how it will puzzle Dr. Maund, when he is sent for to see you! 'My dear Madam, I'm very sorry to say your little girl has got no health at all! I never saw such a thing in my life!' 'Oh, I can easily explain it!' your mother will say. 'You see she would go and make friends with a strange gentleman, and yesterday he drank her health!' 'Well, Mrs. Chataway,' he will say, 'the only way to cure her is to wait till his next birthday, and then for her to drink his health.'

And then we shall have changed healths. I wonder how you'll like mine! Oh, Gertrude, I wish you wouldn't talk such nonsense!

Your loving friend,
Lewis Carroll

To Gertrude Chataway

(Christ Church, Oxford, 9 December 1875)

My dear Gertrude,—This really will not do, you know, sending one more kiss every time by post: the parcel gets so heavy it is quite expensive. When the postman brought in the last letter, he looked quite grave. 'Two pounds to pay, sir!' he said. 'Extra weight, sir!' (I think he cheats a little, by the way. He often makes me pay two pounds, when I think it should be pence). 'Oh, if you please, Mr. Postman!' I said, going down gracefully on one knee (I wish you could see me go down on one knee to a postman—it's a very pretty sight), 'do excuse me just this once! It's only from a little girl!'

'Only from a little girl!' he growled. 'What are little girls made of?' 'Sugar and spice,' I began to say, 'and all that's ni—' but he interrupted me. 'No! I don't mean that. I mean, what's the good of little girls, when they send such heavy letters?' 'Well, they're not much good, certainly,' I said, rather sadly.

'Mind you don't get any more such letters,' he said, 'at

least, not from that particular little girl. I know her well, and she's a regular bad one!' That's not true, is it? I don't believe he ever saw you, and you're not a bad one, are you? However, I promised him we would send each other very few more letters—'Only two thousand four hundred and seventy, or so,' I said. 'Oh!' he said, 'a little number like that doesn't signify. What I meant is, you mustn't send many.'

So you see we must keep count now, and when we get to two thousand four hundred and seventy, we mustn't write any more, unless the postman gives us leave.

I sometimes wish I was back on the shore at Sandown; don't you?

Your loving friend,
Lewis Carroll.

Why is a pig that has lost its tail like a little girl on the seashore?
Because it says, 'I should like another tale, please!'

Old love letters are best remembered

7

Leo Tolstoy to Valeria Arsenev

Count Lev Nikolayevich Tolstoy, popularly known as Leo Tolstoy, was a Russian writer, who is regarded as one of the greatest authors of all time. He was nominated for the Nobel Prize in Literature every year from 1902 to 1906 and for the Noble Peace Prize in 1902 and 1909. The fact that he never won was a major controversy.

He and Valeria Arsenev were engaged to each other when he wrote this letter to her. However, they broke off a while later, and Tolstoy joined the army.

His thoughts on love are vivid and clear: 'To love means in general to do good.'

(2 November 1856)

I already love in you your beauty, but I am only beginning to love in you that which is eternal and ever precious—your heart, your soul.

Beauty one could get to know and fall in love with in one hour and cease to love it as speedily; but the soul one must learn to know. Believe me, nothing on earth is given without labour, even love, the most beautiful and natural of feelings.

Old love letters are best remembered

8

Robert Browning to Elizabeth Barrett Browning

Robert Browning was an English poet, regarded as one of the preeminent Victorian poets of the time. He was known for his dark humour.

Robert Browning and Elizabeth Barrett Browning met and fell in love. Due to the disapproval of Elizabeth's father to their relationship, both eloped and got married. They spent a full fifteen years with each other, enjoying marital bliss, until Elizabeth died in her husband's arms in 1861.

He once said: 'Love is the energy of life.' His statements on love spell his thoughts clearly: 'I was made and meant to look for you and wait for you and become yours forever.'

(11 January 1846, Sunday)

I have no words for you, my dearest,—I shall never have—You are mine, I am yours. Now, here is one sign of what I said: that I must love you more than at first... a little sign, and to be looked narrowly for or it escapes me, but then the increase it shows can only be little, so very little now [...] At first I only thought of being happy in you,—in your happiness: now I most think of you in the dark hours that must come—I shall grow old with you, and die with you—as far as I can look into the night I see the light with me: and surely with that provision of comfort one should turn with fresh joy and renewed sense of security to the sunny middle of the day,—I am in the full sunshine now,—and after, all seems cared for—is it too homely an illustration if I say the day's visit is not crossed by uncertainties as to the return thro' the wild country at nightfall?—

Now Keats speaks of 'Beauty—that must die—and Joy whose hand is ever at his lips, bidding farewell.' And who spoke of—looking up into the eyes and asking 'And how long will you love us'?—There is a Beauty that will not die, a Joy that bids no farewell, dear dearest eyes that will love forever! And I—am to love no longer than I can—Well, dear—and when I can no longer—you will not blame me?—you will do only as ever, kindly and justly,—hardly more: I do not pretend to say I have chosen to put my fancy to such an experiment, and consider how that is to happen, and what measures ought to be taken in the emergency—because in the 'universality of my sympathies' I certainly number a very lively one with my own heart and soul, and cannot amuse myself by such a spectacle as their supposed extinction or paralysis,—there is no doubt I should be an object for the deepest commiseration of you or any more fortunate human being:—and I hope that because such a calamity does not obtrude itself on me as a thing to be prayed against, it is no less duly implied with all the other visitations from which no humanity can be altogether exempt—just as God bids us ask for the continuance of the 'daily bread',—'battle, murder and sudden death' lie behind doubtless—I repeat, and perhaps in so doing, only give one more example of the instantaneous conversion of that indignation we bestow in another's case, into wonderful lenity when it becomes our own, ... that I only contemplate the possibility you make me recognize, with pity, and fear ... no anger at all,—and imprecations of vengeance, for what?—Observe, I only speak of cases possible; of sudden impotency of mind,—that is possible—there are other ways of 'changing', 'ceasing to love' &c which it is safest not to think of nor believe in...

[...]

And now, love, dear heart of my heart, my own, only Ba—see no more—see what I am, what God in his constant mercy ordinarily grants to those who have, as I, received already so much,—much, past expression! It is but...if you will so please—at worst, forestalling the one or two years, for my sake; for you will be as sure of me one day as I can be now of myself—and why not now be sure? See, love—a year is gone by—we were in one relation when you wrote at the end of a letter 'Do not say I do not tire you' (by writing—'I am sure I do'—A year has gone by—Did you tire me then? Now, you tell me what is told; for my sake, sweet, let the few years go by,—we are married—and my arms are round you, and my face touches yours, and I am asking you, 'Were you not to me, in that dim beginning of 1846, a joy beyond all joys, a life added to and transforming mine, the good I choose from all the possible gifts of God on this earth, for which I seem to have lived,—which accepting, I thankfully step aside and let the rest get what they can,—of what, it is very likely, they esteem more—for why should my eye be evil because God's is good,—why should I grudge that, giving them, I do believe, infinitely less, he gives them a content in the inferior good and belief in its worth—I should have wished that further concession, that illusion as I believe it, for their sakes—but I cannot undervalue my own treasure and so scant the only tribute of mere gratitude which is in my power to pay."—Hear this said now before the few years, and believe in it now, for then, dearest!

⌁

Old love letters are best remembered

9

Zelda Fitzgerald to F. Scott Fitzgerald

Zelda Fitzgerald was an American novelist, socialite, painter and playwright. She was popularly called the 'first American Flapper' and was known for her beauty.

F. Scott Fitzgerald and Zelda met each other in 1918 at a dance in Montgomery and Scott fell in love with her. Their love affair was the talk of the town and it symbolized glamour and the Jazz age. They exchanged their love through letters. They married in April 1920.

Fitzgerald once wrote: 'I love her and it is the beginning of everything.' Further, he defines love as a unique experience not comparable with another: 'There are all kinds of love in this world but never the same twice.' Great love letters are never forgotten, and a quote of his can be applied to this sentiment: 'So we beat on boats against the currents, borne back ceaselessly into the past.'

(Spring 1919)

Sweetheart,

Please, please don't be so depressed—We'll be married soon, and then these lonesome nights will be over forever—and until we are, I am loving, loving every tiny minute of the day and night—Maybe you won't understand this, but sometimes when I miss you most, it's hardest to write—and you always know when I make myself—Just the ache of it all—and I can't tell you. If we were together, you'd feel how strong it is—you're so sweet when you're melancholy. I love your sad tenderness—when I've hurt you—That's one of the reasons I could never be sorry for our quarrels—and they bothered you so—Those dear, dear little fusses, when I always tried so hard to make you kiss and forget—

Scott—there's nothing in all the world I want but you—and your precious love—All the material things are nothing. I'd just hate to live a sordid, colorless existence—because you'd soon love me less—and less—and I'd do anything—anything—to keep your heart for my own—I don't want to live—I want to love first, and live incidentally—Why don't you feel that I'm waiting—I'll come to you, Lover, when you're ready—Don't don't ever think of the things you can't give me—You've trusted me with the dearest heart of all—and it's so damn much more than anybody else in all the world has ever had—

How can you think deliberately of life without me—If you should die—O Darling—darling Scott—It'd be like going blind. I know I would, too—I'd have no purpose in life—just a pretty—decoration. Don't you think I was made for you? I feel like you had me ordered—and I was delivered to you—to

be worn—I want you to wear me, like a watch—charm or a button hole boquet (sic)—to the world. And then, when we're alone, I want to help—to know that you can't do anything without me.
[...]

All my heart—
I love you

Old love letters are best remembered

10

William Congreve to Arabella Hunt

William Congreve was a dramatist, who was mainly responsible for a unique genre of drama known as 'Comedy of Errors.' His play The Way of the World *is regarded as one of the best Restoration comedies. He met and fell in love with celebrated musician and a favourite of Queen Mary, Arabella Hunt. Their affair did not consummate into marriage, but the letters William wrote to Arabella are a testament to his love for her.*

Congreve once wrote: 'If there's delight in love, 'tis when I see that heart, which others bleed for, bleed for me.'

Dear Madam,

Not believe that I love you? You cannot pretend to be so incredulous. If you do not believe my tongue, consult my eyes, consult your own. You will find by yours that they have charms; by mine that I have a heart which feels them.

Recall to mind what happened last night. That at least was a love's kiss. Its eagerness, its fierceness, its warmth, expressed the God its parent. But oh! its sweetness, and its melting softness expressed him more. With trembling in my limbs, and fevers in my soul I ravish'd it. Convulsions, pantings, murmurings shew'd the mighty disorder within me: the mighty disorder increased by it. For those dear lips shot through my heart, and thro' my bleeding vitals, delicious poison, and an avoidless but yet a charming ruin.

What cannot a day produce? The night before I thought myself a happy man, in want of nothing, and in fairest expectation of fortune; approved of by men of wit, and applauded by others. Pleased, nay charmed with my friends, my then dearest friends, sensible of every delicate pleasure, and in their turn possessing all.

But Love, almighty Love, seems in a moment to have removed me to a prodigious distance from every object but you alone. In the midst of crowds I remain in solitude. Nothing but you can lay hold of my mind, and that can lay hold of nothing but you. I appear transported to some foreign desert with you (oh, that I were really thus transported!), where, abundantly supplied with everything, in thee, I might live out an age of uninterrupted ecstasy.

The scene of the world's great stage seems suddenly and sadly chang'd. Unlovely objects are all around me, excepting thee; the charms of all the world appear to be translated to thee. Thus in this sad but oh, too pleasing state! my soul can fix upon nothing but thee; thee it contemplates, admires, adores, nay depends on, trusts on you alone.

If you and hope forsake it, despair and endless misery attend it.

Old love letters are best remembered

11

Oscar Wilde to Lord Alfred 'Bosie' Douglas

Oscar Fingal O'Flahertie Wills Wilde was an Irish poet and one of the most renowned playwrights in London. He is best known for his epigrams and plays.

Wilde once wrote: 'I like men who have a future and women who have a past.'

In a lighter vein, he also said: 'Men always want to be a woman's first love, women like to be a man's last romance.'

(January 1893)

My Own Boy,

Your sonnet is quite lovely, and it is a marvel that those red rose-leaf lips of yours should be made no less for the madness of music and song than for the madness of kissing. Your slim gilt soul walks between passion and poetry. I know Hyacinthus, whom Apollo loved so madly, was you in Greek days.

Why are you alone in London, and when do you go to Salisbury? Do go there to cool your hands in the grey twilight of Gothic things, and come here whenever you like. It is a lovely place and lacks only you; but go to Salisbury first.

Always, with undying love, yours,
Oscar

(March 1893)

Dearest of All Boys—Your letter was delightful—red and yellow wine to me—but I am sad and out of sorts—Bosie—you must not make scenes with me—they kill me—they wreck the loveliness of life—I cannot see you, so Greek and gracious, distorted with passion; I cannot listen to your curved lips saying hideous things to me—don't do it—you break my heart—I'd sooner be rented all day, than have you bitter, unjust, and horrid—horrid.

I must see you soon—you are the divine thing I want—the thing of grace and genius—but but I don't know how to do it—Shall I come to Salisbury—? There are many difficulties—my bill here is £49 for a week! I have also got a new sitting-room over the Thames—but you, why are you not here, my dear, my wonderful boy—? I fear I must leave; no money, no credit, and a heart of lead—

Ever your own,
Oscar

(December 1893)

My dearest Boy,

Thanks for your letter. I am overwhelmed by the wings of vulture creditors, and out of sorts, but I am happy in the knowledge that we are friends again, and that our love has passed through the shadow and the light of estrangement and sorrow and come out rose-crowned as of old. Let us always be infinitely dear to each other, as indeed we have been always.
 I think of you daily, and am always devotedly yours.

Oscar

(July 1894)

My own dear Boy,

I hope the cigarettes arrived all right. I lunched with Gladys de Grey, Reggie and Aleck York there. They want me to go to Paris with them on Thursday: they say one wears flannels and straw hats and dines in the Bois, but, of course, I have no money, as usual, and can't go. Besides, I want to see you. It is really absurd. I can't live without you. You are so dear, so wonderful. I think of you all day long, and miss your grace, your boyish beauty, the bright sword-play of your wit, the delicate fancy of your genius, so surprising always in its sudden swallow-flights towards north and south, towards sun and moon—and, above all, yourself. The only thing that consoles me is what Sybil of Mortimer Street (whom mortals call Mrs. Robinson) said to me. If I could disbelieve her I would, but I can't, and I know that early in January you and I will go away together for a long voyage, and that your lovely life goes always hand in hand with mine. My dear wonderful boy, I hope you are brilliant and happy.

I went to Bertie, today I wrote at home, then went and sat with my mother. Death and Love seem to walk on either hand as I go through life: they are the only things I think of, their wings shadow me.

London is a desert without your dainty feet... Write me a line and take all my love—now and for ever.

Always, and with devotion—but I have no words for how I love you.

Oscar

(29 April 1895)

My dearest boy,

This is to assure you of my immortal, my eternal love for you. Tomorrow all will be over. If prison and dishonour be my destiny, think that my love for you and this idea, this still more divine belief, that you love me in return will sustain me in my unhappiness and will make me capable, I hope, of bearing my grief most patiently. Since the hope, nay rather the certainty, of meeting you again in some world is the goal and the encouragement of my present life, ah! I must continue to live in this world because of that.

(31 August 1897, Tuesday, 7:30)

My own Darling Boy,

I got your telegram half an hour ago, and just send a line to say that I feel that my only hope of again doing beautiful work in art is being with you. It was not so in the old days, but now it is different, and you can really recreate in me that energy and sense of joyous power on which art depends. Everyone is furious with me for going back to you, but they don't understand us. I feel that it is only with you that I can do anything at all. Do remake my ruined life for me, and then our friendship and love will have a different meaning to the world.

    I wish that when we met at Rouen we had not parted at all. There are such wide abysses now of space and land between us. But we love each other. Goodnight, dear. Ever yours,

Oscar

Old love letters are best remembered

12

Emma Darwin to Charles Darwin

Emma Darwin was the first cousin and wife of Charles Darwin, who was an English biologist, geologist and naturalist, known for his theory of evolution. Charles Darwin once wrote: 'the love for all living creatures is the most noble attribute of man.'

I cannot tell you the compassion I have felt for all your sufferings for these weeks past that you have had so many drawbacks. Nor the gratitude I have felt for the cheerful & affectionate looks you have given me when I know you have been miserably uncomfortable.

My heart has often been too full to speak or take any notice. I am sure you know I love you well enough to believe that I mind your sufferings nearly as much as I should my own & I find the only relief to my own mind is to take it as from God's hand, & to try to believe that all suffering & illness is meant to help us to exalt our minds & to look forward with hope to a future state. When I see your patience, deep compassion for others self command & above all gratitude for the smallest thing done to help you I cannot help longing that these precious feelings should be offered to Heaven for the sake of your daily happiness. But I find it difficult enough in my own case. I often think of the words 'Thou shalt keep him in perfect peace whose mind is stayed on thee.' It is feeling & not reasoning that drives one to prayer. I feel presumptuous in writing thus to you.

I feel in my inmost heart your admirable qualities & feelings & all I would hope is that you might direct them upwards, as well as to one who values them above every thing in the world. I shall keep this by me till I feel cheerful & comfortable again about you but it has passed through my mind often lately so I thought I would write it partly to relieve my own mind.

Old love letters are best remembered

13

Napoleon Bonaparte to Joséphine de Beauharnais

Napoleon Bonaparte was a French military general and regarded as the one of the greatest military leaders of the world. He was also the first emperor of France.

Napoleon once wrote: 'I must see her and press her to my heart. I love her to the point of madness and I cannot continue to be separated from her.'

(November 1796)

I am going to bed with my heart full of your adorable image... I cannot wait to give you proofs of my ardent love... How happy I would be if I could assist you at your undressing, the little firm white breast, the adorable face, the hair tied up in a scarf a la creole. You know that I will never forget the little visits, you know, the little black forest... I kiss it a thousand times and wait impatiently for the moment I will be in it. To live within Josephine is to live in the Elysian fields. Kisses on your mouth, your eyes, your breast, everywhere, everywhere.

Napoleon Bonaparte to Joséphine de Beauharnais

(17 July 1796)

I got your letter, my beloved; it has filled my heart with joy. I am grateful to you for the trouble you have taken to send me news; your health should be better to-day—I am sure you are cured. I urge you strongly to ride, which cannot fail to do you good.

Ever since I left you, I have been sad. I am only happy when by your side. Ceaselessly I recall your kisses, your tears, your enchanting jealousy; and the charms of the incomparable Joséphine keep constantly alight a bright and burning flame in my heart and senses. When, free from every worry, from all business, shall I spend all my moments by your side, to have nothing to do but to love you, and to prove it to you? I shall send your horse, but I am hoping that you will soon be able to rejoin me. I thought I loved you some days ago; but, since I saw you, I feel that I love you even a thousand times more. Ever since I have known you, I worship you more every day; which proves how false is the maxim of La Bruyère that 'Love comes all at once.' Everything in nature has a regular course, and different degrees of growth.

Ah! pray let me see some of your faults; be less beautiful, less gracious, less tender, and, especially less kind; above all never be jealous, never weep; your tears madden me, fire my blood. Be sure that it is no longer possible for me to have a thought except for you, or an idea of which you shall not be the judge.

Have a good rest. Haste to get well. Come and join me, so that, at least, before dying, we could say—'We were happy for so many days!!'

Millions of kisses, and even to Fortuné, in spite of his naughtiness.

(1796)

I have not spent a day without loving you; I have not spent a night without embracing you; I have not so much as drunk a single cup of tea without cursing the pride and ambition which force me to remain separated from the moving spirit of my life.

In the midst of my duties, whether I am at the head of my army or inspecting the camps, my beloved Josephine stands alone in my heart, occupies my mind, fills my thoughts.

If I am moving away from you with the speed of the Rhone torrent, it is only that I may see you again more quickly.

If I rise to work in the middle of the night, it is because this may hasten by a matter of days the arrival of my sweet love.

Yet in your letter of the 23rd, and 26th. Ventose, you call me vous. Vous yourself!

Ah! wretch, how could you have written this letter? How cold it is?

And then there are those four days between the 23rd, and the 26th.; what were you doing that you failed to write to your husband? ...

Ah, my love, that vous, those four days made me long for my former indifference. Woe to the person responsible!

May he as punishment and penalty, experience what my convictions and the evidence (which is in your friend's favour) would make me experience!

Hell has no torments great enough! Nor do the Furies have serpents enough! Vous! Vous!

Ah! how will things stand in two weeks? ...My spirit is heavy; my heart is fettered and I am terrified by my fantasies...

You love me less; but you will get over the loss. One day you will love me no longer; at least tell me; then I shall know how I have come to deserve this misfortune. ...Farewell, my wife: the torment, joy, hope and moving which draw me close to Nature, and with violent impulses as tumultuous as thunder. I ask of you neither eternal love, nor fidelity, but simply...truth, unlimited honesty.

The day when you say 'I love you less', will mark the end of my love and the last day of my life.

If my heart were base enough to love without being loved in return I would tear it to pieces.

Josephine! Josephine! Remember what I have sometimes said to you: Nature has endowed me with a virile and decisive character. It has built yours out of lace and gossamer. Have you ceased to love me?

Forgive me, love of my life, my soul is racked by conflicting forces. My heart obsessed by you, is full of fears which prostrate me with misery...I am distressed not to be calling you by name. I shall wait for you to write it.

Farewell! Ah! if you love me less you can never have loved me. In that case I shall truly be pitiable.

Bonaparte

P.S. The war this year has changed beyond recognition. I have had meat, bread and fodder distributed; my armed cavalry will soon be on the march.

My soldiers are showing inexpressible confidence in me; you alone are a source of chagrin to me; you alone are the joy and torment of my life.

I send a kiss to your children, whom you do not mention. By God! If you did, your letters would be half as long again. Then visitors at ten o'clock in the morning would not have the pleasure of seeing you. Woman!!!

(Spring 1797)

I love you no longer; on the contrary, I detest you. you are a wretch, truly perverse, truly stupid, a real Cinderella. You never write to me at all, you do not love your husband; you know the pleasure that your letters give him yet you cannot even manage to write him half a dozen lines, dashed off in a moment! What then do you do all day, Madame? What business is so vital that it robs you of the time to write to your faithful lover? What attachment can be stifling and pushing aside the love, the tender and constant love which you promised him? Who can this wonderful new lover be who takes up your every moment, rules your days and prevents you from devoting your attention to your husband?

Beware, Josephine; one fine night the doors will be broken down and there I shall be. In truth, I am worried, my love, to have no news from you; write me a four page letter instantly made up from those delightful words which fill my heart with emotion and joy. I hope to hold you in my arms before long, when I shall lavish upon you a million kisses, burning as the equatorial sun.

Old love letters are best remembered

14

Sir Walter Raleigh to Elizabeth Raleigh

Sir Walter Raleigh was executed in 1618. Sentenced to death for treason on 17 November 1603, he wrote this letter to his wife in December, fearing he would be executed as early as the next day.

Raleigh, in his inimitable style, wrote with a plethora of emotions: the inflections ranging from tender to bitter, from realistic to devotional. The subtle nuances of his mood swings in the letter lay bare his anger, pride and self-importance.

This letter reveals Raleigh at his most vulnerable, with his fear and desire to cling to life apparent in its heartbreaking sign-off.

(December 1603)

You shall now receive (my dear wife) my last words in these my last lines. My love I send you, that you may keep it when I am dead, and my counsel that you may remember it when I am no more. I would not by my will present you with sorrows (dear Bess). Let them go to the grave with me and be buried in the dust. And seeing that it is not the will of God that I should see you any more in this life, bear it patiently, and with a heart like thy self.

First, I send you all the thanks which my heart can conceive, or my words can express for your many travails, and care taken for me, which, though they have not taken effect as you wished, yet my debt to you is not the less: but pay it I never shall in this world.

Secondly, I beseech you for the love you bear me living, do not hide your self many days, but by your travails seek to help your miserable fortunes and the right of your poor child. Thy mourning cannot avail me, I am but dust.

Thirdly, you shall understand, that my land was conveyed *bona fide* to my child: the writings were drawn at midsummer twelve months. My honest cousin Brett can testify so much, and Dalberry, too, can remember somewhat therein. And I trust that my blood will quench their malice that have thus cruelly murthered me: and that they will not seek also to kill thee and thine with extreme poverty. To what friend to direct thee I know not, for all mine have left me in the true time of trial. And I plainly perceive that my death was determined from the first day.

Most sorry I am, God knows, that being thus surprised with death I can leave you in no better estate. God is my witness I meant you all my office of wines or all that I could have purchased by selling it, half of my stuff, and all my jewels, but some on it for the boy. But God hath prevented all my resolutions, and even great God that ruleth all in all. But if you live free from want, care for no more, for the rest is but vanity.

Love God, and begin betimes to repose your self upon him, and therein shall you find true and lasting riches, and endless comfort: for the rest when you have travailed and wearied your thoughts over all sorts of worldly cogitations, you shall but sit down by sorrow in the end. Teach your son also to love and fear God whilst he is yet young, that the fear of God may grow with him, and the same God will be a husband to you, and a father to him; a husband and a father which cannot be taken from you.

Baylie oweth me 200 pounds, and Adrian Gilbert 600. In Jersey I also have much owing me besides. The arrearages of the wines will pay my debts. And howsoever you do, for my soul's sake, pay all poor men. When I am gone, no doubt you shall be sought for by many, for the world thinks that I was very rich. But take heed of the pretences of men, and their affections, for they last not, but in honest and worthy men, and no greater misery can befall you in this life, than to become a prey, and afterwards to be despised. I speak not this (God knows) to dissuade you from marriage, for it will be best for you, both in respect of the world and of God.

As for me, I am no more yours, nor you mine. Death hath cut us asunder and God hath divided me from the world, and you from me. Remember your poor child for his father's sake, who chose you, and loved you in his happiest times.

Get those letters (if it be possible) which I writ to the Lords, wherein I sued for my life. God is my witness, it was for you and yours that I desired life. But it is true that I disdained my self for begging of it. For know it (my dear wife) that your son is the son of a true man, and one who in his own respect despiseth death and all his misshapen and ugly formes.

I cannot write much. God he knows how hardly I steal this time while others sleep, and it is also time that I should separate my thoughts from the world. Beg my dead body which living was denied thee; and either lay it at Sherburne (and if the land continue) or in Exeter-Church, by my father and mother. I can say no more, time and death call me away.

The everlasting God, powerful, infinite, and omnipotent God, that almighty God, who is goodness it self, the true life and true light keep thee and thine. Have mercy on me, and teach me to forgive my persecutors and false accusers, and send us to meet in his glorious kingdom.

My dear wife farewell. Bless my poor boy. Pray for me, and let my good God hold you both in his arms. Written with the dying hand of sometimes thy husband, but now alas overthrown.

Yours that was, but now not my own.
WR

Old love letters are best remembered

15

Lord Byron to Teresa Guiccioli

George Gordon Byron, popularly known as Lord Byron, is regarded as one of the greatest English Romantic poets. He once wrote: 'in her first passion, a woman loves her lover, in all the others, all she loves is love.'

(August 1819)

My dearest Teresa,

I have read this book in your garden;—my love, you were absent, or else I could not have read it. It is a favourite book of yours, and the writer was a friend of mine. You will not understand these English words, and others will not understand them,—which is the reason I have not scrawled them in Italian. But you will recognize the handwriting of him who passionately loved you, and you will divine that, over a book which was yours, he could only think of love.

In that word, beautiful in all languages, but most so in yours—Amor mio—is comprised my existence here and hereafter. I feel I exist here, and I feel I shall exist hereafter,—to what purpose you will decide; my destiny rests with you, and you are a woman, eighteen years of age, and two out of a convent. I love you, and you love me,—at least, you say so, and act as if you did so, which last is a great consolation in all events.

But I more than love you, and cannot cease to love you. Think of me, sometimes, when the Alps and ocean divide us,—but they never will, unless you wish it.

Old love letters are best remembered

16

Henry VIII to Anne Boleyn

Henry VIII was the King of England from 1509 to 1547 (till his death). In William Shakespeare's play, Henry VIII recites the incredible line, 'My drops of tears I will turn to sparks of fire.'

(c. August 1528)

MY MISTRESS & FRIEND,

my heart and I surrender ourselves into your hands, beseeching you to hold us commended to your favour, and that by absence your affection to us may not be lessened: for it were a great pity to increase our pain, of which absence produces enough and more than I could ever have thought could be felt, reminding us of a point in astronomy which is this: the longer the days are, the more distant is the sun, and nevertheless the hotter; so is it with our love, for by absence we are kept a distance from one another, and yet it retains its fervour, at least on my side; I hope the like on yours, assuring you that on my part the pain of absence is already too great for me; and when I think of the increase of that which I am forced to suffer, it would be almost intolerable, but for the firm hope I have of your unchangeable affection for me: and to remind you of this sometimes, and seeing that I cannot be personally present with you, I now send you the nearest thing I can to that, namely, my picture set in a bracelet, with the whole of the device, which you already know, wishing myself in their place, if it should please you.

This is from the hand of your loyal servant and friend,

H. R.

TO MY MISTRESS.

Because the time seems very long since I heard concerning your health and you, the great affection I have for you has induced me to send you this bearer, to be better informed of your health and pleasure, and because, since my parting from you, I have been told that the opinion in which I left you is totally changed, and that you would not come to court either with your mother, if you could, or in any other manner; which report, if true, I cannot sufficiently marvel at, because I am sure that I have since never done any thing to offend you, and it seems a very poor return for the great love which I bear you to keep me at a distance both from the speech and the person of the woman that I esteem most in the world: and if you love me with as much affection as I hope you do, I am sure that the distance of our two persons would be a little irksome to you, though this does not belong so much to the mistress as to the servant.

Consider well, my mistress, that absence from you grieves me sorely, hoping that it is not your will that it should be so; but if I knew for certain that you voluntarily desired it, I could do no other than mourn my ill-fortune, and by degrees abate my great folly. And so, for lack of time, I make an end of this rude letter, beseeching you to give credence to this bearer in all that he will tell you from me.

Written by the hand of your entire Servant,

H. R.

Old love letters are best remembered

17

Benjamin Franklin to Anne Brillon

Benjamin Franklin was an American author, scientist, inventor, publisher, printer and diplomat. He helped in the drafting of the Declaration of Independence.

He once wrote: 'Where there is marriage without love, there will be love without marriage.' Further, he wrote: 'Love and toothache have many cures, but none infallible, except possession and dispossession.'

Madame Brillon,

What a difference, my dear friend, between you and me! You find innumerable faults with me, whereas I see only one fault in you (but perhaps that is the fault of my glasses). I mean this kind of avarice which leads you to seek monopoly on all my affection, and not allow me any for the agreeable ladies of your country.

Do you imagine that it is impossible for my affection (or my tenderness) to be divided without being diminished? You deceive yourself, and you forget the playful manner with which you stopped me. You renounce and totally exclude all that might be of the flesh in our affection, allowing me only some kisses, civil and honest, such as you might grant your little cousins. What am I receiving that is so special as to prevent me from giving the same to others, without taking from what belongs to you?

The sweet sounds brought forth from the pianoforte by your clever hand can be enjoyed by twenty people simultaneously without diminishing at all the pleasure you so obligingly mean for me, and I could, with as little reason, demand from your affection that no other ears but mine be allowed to be charmed by those sweet sounds.

Yours,
Benjamin

Old love letters are best remembered

18

Robert Burns to Agnes Maclehose

Love letters are made of poetic emotions and passion that paints the pages. Sometimes the prose is expressed in poetry or verse. What could be a better example than the poem by Robert Burns:

A Red, Red Rose

O my luve's like a red, red rose.
That's newly sprung in June;
O my luve's like a melodie
That's sweetly play'd in tune.
As fair art thou, my bonnie lass,
So deep in luve am I;
And I will love thee still, my Dear,
Till a'the seas gang dry.
Till a' the seas gang dry, my Dear,
And the rocks melt wi' the sun:
I will luve thee still, my Dear,
While the sands o'life shall run.
And fare thee weel my only Luve!
And fare thee weel a while!
And I will come again, my Luve,
Tho' it were ten thousand mile!

(25 January 1788)

Clarinda, my life, you have wounded my soul. Can I think of your being unhappy, even tho' it be not described in your pathetic elegance of language, without being miserable?

Clarinda, can I bear to be told from you, that 'you will not see me tomorrow night'—that you 'wish the hour of parting were come'! Do not let us impose on ourselves by sounds: if in the moment of fond endearment and tender dalliance, I perhaps trespassed against the letter of Decorum's law; I appeal, even to you, whether I ever sinned in the very least degree against the spirit of her strictest statute.

But why, My Love, talk to me in such strong terms; every word of which cuts me to the very soul? You know, a hint, the slightest signification of your wish, is to me a sacred command.

Be reconciled, My Angel, to your God, your self and me; and I pledge you Sylvander's honour, an oath I dare say you will trust without reserve, that you shall never more have reason to complain of his conduct.

Now, my Love, do not wound our next meeting with any averted looks or restrained caresses: I have marked the line of conduct, a line I know exactly to your taste, and which I will inviolably keep; but do not you show the least inclination to make boundaries: seeming distrust, where you know you may confide, is a cruel sin against Sensibility.

'Delicacy, you know it, was which won me to you at once—take care you do not loosen the dearest most sacred tie that unites us.' Clarinda, I would not have stung your soul, I would not have bruised your spirit, as that harsh crucifying, 'Take care,' did mine; no, not to have gained heaven! Let me again appeal to your dear Self, if Sylvander, even when he seemingly half-transgressed the laws of Decorum, if he did not shew more chastised, trembling, faltering delicacy, than the MANY of the world do in keeping these laws.

O Love and Sensibility, ye have conspired against My Peace! I love to madness, and I feel to torture! Clarinda, how can I forgive myself, that I ever have touched a single chord in your bosom with pain! would I do it willingly? Would any consideration, any gratification make me do so?

O, did you love like me, you would not, you could not deny or put off a meeting with the Man who adores you; who would die a thousand deaths before he would injure you; and who must soon bid you a long farewell! I had proposed bringing my bosom friend, Mr. Ainslie, tomorrow evening, at his strong request, to see you; as he only has time to stay with us about ten minutes, for an engagement; but-I shall hear from you: this afternoon, for mercy's sake! for till I hear from you I am wretched. O Clarinda, the tie that binds me to thee, is entwisted, incorporated with my dearest threads of life!

SYLVANDER.

Old love letters are best remembered

19

Nathaniel Hawthorne to Sophia Peabody

Nathaniel Hawthorne was an American novelist and a short story writer.

He once quoted: 'Love, whether newly born or aroused from a death like slumber, must always create sunshine, filling the heart so full of radiance, that it overflows upon the outward world.'

(5 December 1839)

Dearest,—I wish your husband had the gift of making rhymes, for methinks there is poetry in my head and heart since I have been in love with you. You are a Poem. Of what sort, then? Epic? Mercy on me, no! A sonnet? No; for that is too labored and artificial. You are a sort of sweet, simple, gay, pathetic ballad, which Nature is singing, sometimes with tears, sometimes with smiles, and sometimes with intermingled smiles and tears.

(Salem, 10 September 1841)

Dear Miss Peabody,

Most dear wife, thou canst not imagine how strange it seems to me that thou shouldst ever suffer any bodily harm. I cannot conceive of it—the idea will not take the aspect of reality. Thou art to me a spirit gliding about our familiar paths: and I always feel as if thou wert beyond the reach of mortal accident—nor am I convinced to the contrary even by thy continual gashings of thy dearest fingers and sprainings of thy ancle (sic). I love thee into the next state of existence, and therefore do not realise that thou art here as subject to corporeal harm as is thy husband himself—nay, ten times more so, because thy earthly manifestation is refined almost into spirit.

But, dearest, thy accident did make thy husband's heart flutter very riotously. I wanted to hold thee in mine arms; for I had a foolish notion that thou wouldst be much better—perhaps quite well! I cannot tell thee all I felt; and still I had not the horrible feelings that I should expect, because there was a shadowiness interposed between me and the fact, so that it did not strike my heart, as the beam did thy head. Let me not speak of it anymore, lest it become too real.

Sweetest, thou dost please me much by criticising thy husband's stories, and finding fault with them. I do not very well recollect Monsieur de Miroir; but as to Mrs. Bullfrog, I give her up to thy severest reprehension. The story was written as a mere experiment in that style; it did not come from am depth within me—neither my heart nor mind had anything to do with it. I recollect that the Man of Adamant seemed a fine idea to me, when I looked at it prophetically; but I failed in giving shape and substance to the vision which I saw. I don't think it can be very good.

Ownest wife, I cannot believe all these stories about Munroe, because such an abominable rascal never would be sustained and countenanced by respectable men. I take him to be neither better nor worse than the average of his tribe. However, I intend to have all my copy-rights taken out in my own name; and if he cheats me once, I will have nothing more to do with him, but will straightway be cheated by some other publisher—that being, of course, the only alternative.

Dearest, what dost thou think of taking Governor Shirley's young French wife as the subject of one of the cuts? Thou shouldst represent her in the great chair, perhaps with a dressing glass before her, and arrayed in all manner of fantastic finery, and with an outré French air; while the old Governor is leaning fondly over her, and a Puritan counsellor or two are manifesting their disgust, in the background. A negro footman and French waiting maid might be in attendance. Do not think that I expect thee to adopt my foolish fancies about these things. Whatever thou mayst do, it will be better than I can think. In Liberty Tree, thou mightest have a vignette, representing the chair in a very battered, shattered, and forlorn condition, after it had been ejected from Hutchinson's house. This would serve to impress the reader with the woeful vicissitudes of sublunary things. Many other subjects would thy husband suggest, but he is terribly afraid that thou wouldst take one of them, instead of working out thine own inspirations.

Belovedest, I long to see thee. Do be magnificently well by Saturday—yet not on my account, but thine own. Meantime, take care of thy dearest head. Thou art not fit to be trusted away from thy husband's guidance, one moment.

Dear little wife, didst thou ever behold such an awful scribble as thy husband writes, since he became a farmer? His chirography always was abominable; but now it is outrageous.

God bless thee, dearest and may His hand be continually outstretched over thy head. Expect me on Saturday afternoon.

THINE OWNEST HUSBAND.

Old love letters are best remembered

20

George Bernard Shaw to Beatrice Campbell

George Bernard Shaw was an Irish critic, playwright, political activist and polemicist. He had a great influence on Western culture, theatre and politics. Commenting on love letters, he wrote: 'The perfect love affair is one which is conducted entirely by post.'

(27 February 1913)

To 'Stella' Beatrice Campbell

[...] I want my rapscallionly fellow vagabond. I want my dark lady. I want my angel—I want my tempter.
 I want my Freia with her apples. I want the lighter of my seven lamps of beauty, honour, laughter, music, love, life and immortality... I want my inspiration, my folly, my happiness, my divinity, my madness, my selfishness, my final sanity and sanctification, my transfiguration, my purification, my light across the sea, my palm across the desert, my garden of lovely flowers, my million nameless joys, my day's wage, my night's dream, my darling and my star. [...]

Old love letters are best remembered

21

Pliny the Younger to Calpurnia

Gaius Plinius Caecilius Secundus, better known as Pliny the Younger, was an author, lawyer and magistrate of Ancient Rome. He once wrote: 'Let me into the secrets you would prefer no one to know.'

⌇

You will not believe what a longing for you possesses me. The chief cause of this is my love; and then we have not grown used to be apart.

So it comes to pass that I lie awake a great part of the night, thinking of you; and that by day, when the hours return at which I was wont to visit you, my feet take me, as it is so truly said, to your chamber, but not finding you there I return, sick and sad at heart, like an excluded lover.

The only time that is free from these torments is when I am being worn out at the bar, and in the suits of my friends. Judge you what must be my life when I find my repose in toil, my solace in wretchedness and anxiety.

Farewell.

⌇

Old love letters are best remembered

22

Marilyn Monroe to Joe DiMaggio

Marilyn Monroe was an American model, actor and singer. She was the Hollywood sex symbol in the 1950s and the 60s. She is still regarded as an icon of pop culture.

She once stated: 'The real lover is the man who can thrill you just by touching your head or smiling into your eyes—or just by staring into space.'

(28 February 1954)

I don't know how to tell you just how much I miss you. I love you till my heart could burst. All I love, all I want, all I need is you—forever. I want to just be where you are and be just what you want me to be.

I know its lousy of me to be so late so often and I promise to try a million times harder, I promise. I want someday for you to be proud of me as a person and as your wife and as the mother of the rest of your children. (two at least! I've decided.)

I miss it so much when you don't love me and hold me and cuddle me to sleep every night. I want to be near you and I feel so sad tonight.

Darling, please don't leave me anymore.

Love, Marilyn

Old love letters are best remembered

23

Richard Steele to Mary Scurlock

Sir Richard Steele was an Anglo-Irish playwright, writer and politician. In a humorous vein, Richard Steele wrote: 'A woman seldom writes her mind but in her postscript.'

(14 August 1707)

MADAM,

I came to your house this night to wait on you; but you have commanded me to expect the happiness of seeing you at another time of more leisure. I am now under your own roof while I write; and that imaginary satisfaction of being so near you, tho' not in your presence, has in it something that touches me with so tender ideas, that it is impossible for me to describe their force. All great passion makes us dumb; and the highest happiness, as well as highest grief, seizes us too violently to be expressed by our words.

You are so good as to let me know I shall have the honour of seeing you when I next come here. I will live upon that expectation, and meditate on your perfections till that happy hour. The vainest woman upon earth never saw in her glasse half the attractions which I view in you. Your air, your shape, your every glance, motion, and gesture, have such peculiar graces, that you possess my whole soul, and I know no life but in the hopes of your approbation: I know not what to say, but that I love you with the sincerest passion that ever entered the heart of man. I will make it the business of my life to find out means of convincing you that I prefer you to all that's pleasing upon earth. I am, Madam, your most obedient, most faithful humble ser'nt.

Old love letters are best remembered

24

James Joyce to Nora Barnacle

James Augustine Aloysius Joyce was an Irish poet, novelist and critic. He once said: 'First we feel. Then we fall. But my body was like a harp and her words and gestures were like fingers.'

(October 1909)

My darling Tonight the old fever of love has begun to wake again in me. I am a shell of a man: my soul is in Trieste. You alone know me and love me.

I am a jealous, lonely, dissatisfied, proud man. Why are you not more patient with me and kinder with me? The night we went to *Madame Butterfly* together you treated me most rudely. I simply wanted to feel your soul swaying with languor and longing as mine did when she sings the romance of her hope in the second act *Un bel di*: 'One day, one day, we shall see a spire of smoke rising on the furthest verge of the sea; and then the ship appears.' I am a little disappointed in you. Then another night I came home to your bed from the café and I began to tell you of all I hoped to do, and to write, in the future and of those boundless ambitions which are really the leading forces in my life. You would not listen to me. It was very late I know and of course you were tired out after the day. But a man whose brain is on fire with hope and trust in himself must tell someone of what he feels. Whom should I tell but you?

I love you deeply and truly, Nora. I feel worthy of you now. There is not a particle of my love that is not yours. In spite of these things which blacken my mind against you I think of you always at your best... Nora, I love you. I cannot live without you. I would like to give you everything that is mine, any knowledge I have (little as it is), any emotions I myself feel or have felt, any likes or dislikes I have, any hopes I have or remorse. I would like to go through life side by side with you, telling you more and more until we grew to be one being together until the hour should come for us to die. Even now the tears rush to my eyes and sobs choke my throat as I write this. Nora, we have only one short life in which to love. O my darling be only a little kinder to me, bear with me a little even if I am inconsiderate and unmanageable and believe me we will be happy together. Let me love you in my own way. Let me have your heart always close to mine to hear every throb of my life, every sorrow, every joy.

Old love letters are best remembered

25

Dylan Thomas to Caitlin Thomas

Dylan Thomas was a Welsh writer and poet, regarded as one of the greatest poets of the twentieth century. Every year in Wales, the Dylan Thomas Festival is organized. There is also a Dylan Thomas Prize awarded to the best published writer under 30.

He once said: 'Why do men think you can pick love up and re-light it like a candle? Women know when love is over.'

(25 February 1950)

My darling far away love, my precious Caitlin, my wife dear, I love you as I have never loved you, oh please remember me all day and every day as I remember you here in this terrible, beautiful, dream and nightmare city which would only be any good at all if we were together in it, if every night we clung together in it. I love you, Cat, my Cat, your body, heart, soul, everything, and I am always and entirely yours.

How are you, my dear? And how is my beloved Colm and sweet fiend Aeron? Give them my love please. And how are the old ones? I'll write to them, too. I love you, I can see you, now this minute, your face and body, your beautiful hair, I can hear your lovely, un- understandable voice. I love you, and I love our children, and I love our house...

Here, each night I have to take things to sleep: I am staying right in the middle of Manhattan, surrounded by skyscrapers infinitely taller and stranger than one has ever known from the pictures: I'm staying in a room, a hotel room for the promised flat did not come off, on the 30th floor: and the noise all day and night: without some drug, I couldn't sleep at all. The hugest, heaviest lorries, police cars, fire-brigades, ambulances, all with their banshee sirens wailing and screaming, seem never to stop, and I have no idea what on earth I am doing here in the very loud, mad middle of the last mad Empire on earth:—except to think of you, and love you, and to work for us.

I have done two readings this week, to the Poetry Centre of New York: each time there was an audience of about a thousand. I felt a very lonely, foreign midget orating up there, in a huge hall, before all those faces; the readings went well.

I've been to a few parties, lots of American poets, writers, critics, hangers on, some very pleasant, all furiously polite and hospitable. But apart from on one occasion, I've stuck nearly all the time to American beer, which, though thin, I like a lot and is ice cold.

I've been, too, to lots of famous places: up to the top of the Empire State Building, the tallest there is, which terrified me so much, I had to come down at once;

And now it must look to you, my Cat, as though I am enjoying myself here. I'm not. It's a nightmare, night and day; there never was such a place: I would never get used to the speed, the noise, the utter indifference of the crowds, the frightening politeness of the intellectuals, and, most of all, these huge phallic towers, up and up and up, hundreds of floors, into the impossible sky.

Old love letters are best remembered

26

Alexander Pope to Martha Blount

Alexander Pope is regarded as one of the most prominent English poets of the eighteenth century. He was also a satirist and a translator. He once said: 'Love, free as air, at sight of human ties, spreads its light wings, and in a moment flies.'

(1714)

Most Divine!—

It is some proof of my sincerity towards you, that I write when I am prepared by drinking to speak truth; and sure a letter after twelve at night must abound with that noble ingredient. That heart must have abundance of flames, which is at once warmed by wine and you: wine awakens and refreshes the lurking passions of the mind, as does the colours diat are sunk in a picture, and brings them out in all their natural glowings. My good qualities have been so frozen and locked up in a dull constitution at all my former sober hours, that it is very astonishing to me, now I am drunk, to find so much virtue in me.

In these overflowings of my heart I pay you my thanks for those two obliging letters you favoured me with of the 18th and 24th instant. That which begins with 'My charming Mr. Pope!' was a delight to me beyond all expression: you have at last entirely gained the conquest over your fair sister.

It is true you are not handsome, for you are a woman, and think you are not: but this good-humour and tenderness for me has a charm that cannot be resisted. That face must needs be irresistible, which was adorned with smiles even when it could not see the coronation. I do suppose you will not show this epistle out of vanity, as I doubt not your sister does all I write to her. Indeed, to correspond with Mr. Pope, may make any one proud who lives under a dejection of heart in the country.

Every one values Mr. Pope, but every one for a different reason: one for his adherence to the Catholic faith; another for his neglect of Popish superstition; one for his grave behaviour, another for his whimsicalness; Mr. Titcomb, for his pretty atheistical jests; Mr. Caryll, for his moral and Christian sentences; Mrs. Teresa, for his reflections on Mrs. Patty; and Mrs. Patty, for his reflections on Mrs. Teresa.

It was but the other day I heard of Mrs. Fermor's being actually and directly married. I wonder how the couple at _____ look, stare, and simper, since that grand secret came out, which they so well concealed before. They concealed it as well as the barber does his utensils, when he goes to trim upon a Sunday, and his towels hang out all the way. You know your Doctor is gone the way of all his patients, and was hard put to it how to dispose of an estate miserably unwieldy and splendidly unuseful to him. Dr. Shadwell lately told a lady, he wondered she could be alive after him: she made answer, she wondered at it too, both because Dr. Radcliffe was dead, and because Dr. Shadwell was alive. I am Your most faithful admirer, friend, servant, any thing, &c.

I send you Gay's poem on the princess. She is very fat. God help her husband.

Alexander Pope

Old love letters are best remembered

27

Eleanor Roosevelt to Lorena Hickok

Eleanor Roosevelt was the longest-serving First Lady of the United States from 4 March 1933 to 12 April 1945, as her husband, President Franklin D. Roosevelt, served four terms. She was also a diplomat and an activist. She once wrote: 'The giving of love is an education in itself.'

(6 March 1933)

Hick, darling

Ah, how good it was to hear your voice. It was so inadequate to try and tell you what it meant. Funny was that I couldn't say je t'aime and je t'adore as I longed to do, but always remember that I am saying it, that I go to sleep thinking of you.

Old love letters are best remembered

28

Vita Sackville-West to Virginia Woolf

Victorian Mary, Lady Nicolson, CH, better known as Vita Sackville-West, was an English novelist, journalist and poet, who was also a prolific diarist and letter writer. She once wrote: 'I have a deeply hidden inarticulate desire for something beyond the daily life.'

(Milan, 21 January 1926)

I am reduced to a thing that wants Virginia. I composed a beautiful letter to you in the sleepless nightmare hours of the night, and it has all gone: I just miss you, in a quite simple desperate human way. You, with all your undumb letters, would never write so elementary a phrase as that; perhaps you wouldn't even feel it. And yet I believe you'll be sensible of a little gap. But you'd clothe it in so exquisite a phrase that it should lose a little of its reality. Whereas with me it is quite stark: I miss you even more than I could have believed; and I was prepared to miss you a good deal. So this letter is really just a squeal of pain. It is incredible how essential to me you have become. I suppose you are accustomed to people saying these things. Damn you, spoilt creature; I shan't make you love me any more by giving myself away like this—But oh my dear, I can't be clever and stand-offish with you: I love you too much for that. Too truly. You have no idea how stand-offish I can be with people I don't love. I have brought it to a fine art. But you have broken down my defenses. And I don't really resent it.

Old love letters are best remembered

29

Lord Byron to Lady Caroline Lamb

George Gordon Byron, popularly known as Lord Byron, is regarded as one of the greatest English Romantic poets. He once wrote: 'You don't love a woman because she is beautiful, but she is beautiful because you love her.'

(August 1812)

My dearest Caroline,

If tears, which you saw & know I am not apt to shed, if the agitation in which I parted from you, agitation which you must have perceived through the whole of this most nervous affair, did not commence till the moment of leaving you approached, if all that I have said & done, & am still but too ready to say & do, have not sufficiently proved what my real feelings are & must be ever towards you, my love, I have no other proof to offer.

    God knows I wish you happy, & when I quit you, or rather when you from a sense of duty to your husband & mother quit me, you shall acknowledge the truth of what I again promise & vow, that no other in word or deed shall ever hold the place in my affection which is & shall be most sacred to you, till I am nothing.

I never knew till that moment, the madness of—my dearest & most beloved friend—I cannot express myself—this is no time for words—but I shall have a pride, a melancholy pleasure, in suffering what you yourself can hardly conceive—for you do not know me.—I am now about to go out with a heavy heart, because—my appearing this Evening will stop any absurd story which the events of today might give rise to—do you think now that I am cold & stern, & artful—will even others think so, will your mother even—that mother to whom we must indeed sacrifice much, more much more on my part, than she shall ever know or can imagine.

'Promises not to love you' ah Caroline it is past promising—but shall attribute all concessions to the proper motive—& never cease to feel all that you have already witnessed—& more than can ever be known but to my own heart—perhaps to yours—May God protect forgive & bless you—ever & even more than ever.

yr. most attached
BYRON

P.S.—These taunts which have driven you to this—my dearest Caroline—were it not for your mother & the kindness of all your connections, is there anything on earth or heaven would have made me so happy as to have made you mine long ago? & not less now than then, but more than ever at this time—you know I would with pleasure give up all here & all beyond the grave for you—& in refraining from this—must my motives be misunderstood—? I care not who knows this—what use is made of it—it is you & to you only that they owe yourself, I was and am yours, freely & most entirely, to obey, to honour, love—& fly with you when, where, & how you yourself might & may determine.

Old love letters are best remembered

30

Victor Hugo to Adele Foucher

Victor Hugo was a French romantic writer and politician, who wrote in a variety of genres and forms in his literary career that spanned over 60 years. He once stated: 'Love is like a tree: it grows by itself, roots itself deeply in our being and continues to flourish over a heart in ruin.'

(Friday evening, 1 March 1822)

After the two delightful evenings spent yesterday and the day before, I shall certainly not go out tonight, but will sit here at home and write to you.

Besides, my Adele, my adorable and adored Adele, what have I not to tell you?

O, God! for two days, I have been asking myself every moment if such happiness is not a dream.

It seems to me that what I feel is not of earth. I cannot yet comprehend this cloudless heaven.

You do not yet know, Adele, to what I had resigned myself. Alas, do I know it myself?

Because I was weak, I fancied I was calm; because I was preparing myself for all the mad follies of despair, I thought

I was courageous and resigned.

Ah! let me cast myself humbly at your feet, you who are so grand, so tender and strong!

I had been thinking that the utmost limit of my devotion could only be the sacrifice of my life; but you, my generous love, were ready to sacrifice for me the repose of yours.

You have been privileged to receive every gift from nature, you have both fortitude and tears.

Oh, Adele, do not mistake these words for blind enthusiasm—enthusiasm for you has lasted all my life, and increased day by day.

My whole soul is yours.

If my entire existence had not been yours, the harmony of my being would have been lost, and I must have died—died inevitably.

These were my meditations, Adele, when the letter that was to bring me hope or else despair arrived.

If you love me, you know what must have been my joy. What I know you may have felt, I will not describe.

My Adele, why is there no word for this but joy? Is it because there is no power in human speech to express such happiness?

The sudden bound from mournful resignation to infinite felicity seemed to upset me. Even now I am still beside myself and sometimes I tremble lest I should suddenly awaken from this dream divine.

Oh, now you are mine! At last you are mine! Soon—in a few months, perhaps, my angel will sleep in my arms, will awaken in my arms, will live there.

All your thoughts at all moments, all your looks will be for me; all my thoughts, all my moments, all my looks, will be for you!

My Adele!
Adieu, my angel, my beloved Adele! Adieu!
I will kiss your hair and go to bed.
Still I am far from you, but I can dream of you.
Soon perhaps you will be at my side.
Adieu; pardon the delirium of your husband who embraces you, and who adores you, both for this life and another.

(1821)

My dearest,

When two souls, which have sought each other for, however long in the throng, have finally found each other...a union, fiery and pure as they themselves are...begins on earth and continues forever in heaven.

This union is love, true love,...a religion, which deifies the loved one, whose life comes from devotion and passion, and for which the greatest sacrifices are the sweetest delights.

This is the love which you inspire in me... Your soul is made to love with the purity and passion of angels; but perhaps it can only love another angel, in which case I must tremble with apprehension.

Yours forever,
Victor Hugo

Old love letters are best remembered

31

Alfred de Musset to George Sand

Alfred Louis Charles de Musset-Pathay was a French novelist, poet, dramatist and a great icon of French history. He once said: 'With a kiss let us set out for an unknown world...'

(1833)

I have something stupid and ridiculous to tell you. I am foolishly writing to you instead of having told you this, I do not know why, when returning from that walk.

To-night I shall be annoyed at having done so. You will laugh in my face, will take me for a maker of phrases in all my relations with you hitherto. You will show me the door and you will think I am lying.

I am in love with you. I have been thus since the first day I called on you.

Old love letters are best remembered

32

Robert Schumann to Clara Wieck

Robert Schumann was a German pianist, composer and an influential music critic. He is known for composing some of the greatest musical works in history and was regarded as a great composer of the Romantic Era.

He once wrote: 'You are like a lighthouse shining beside the sea of humanity, motionless: all you can see is your own reflection in the water. You are alone, so you think...'

(Leizpig, 1838)

Clara,

How happy your last letters have made me—those since Christmas Eve! I should like to call you by all the endearing epithets, and yet I can find no lovelier word than the simple word 'dear,' but there is a particular way of saying it. My dear one, then, I have wept for joy to think that you are mine, and often wonder if I deserve you.

One would think that no one man's heart and brain could stand all the things that are crowded into one day. Where do these thousands of thoughts, wishes, sorrows, joys and hopes come from? Day in, day out, the procession goes on. But how light-hearted I was yesterday and the day before! There shone out of your letters so noble a spirit, such faith, such a wealth of love!

What would I not do for love of you, my own Clara! The knights of old were better off; they could go through fire or slay dragons to win their ladies, but we of today have to content ourselves with more prosaic methods, such as smoking fewer cigars, and the like. After all, though, we can love, knights or no knights; and so, as ever, only the times change, not men's hearts…

You cannot think how your letter has raised and strengthened me… You are splendid, and I have much more reason to be proud of you than you of me. I have made up my mind, though, to read all your wishes in your face. Then you will think, even though you don't say it, that your Robert is a really good sort, that he is entirely yours, and he loves you more than words can say.

You shall indeed have cause to think so in the happy future. I still see you as you looked in your little cap that last evening. I still hear you call me du. Clara, I heard nothing of what you said but that du. Don't you remember?

But I see you in many another unforgettable guise. Once you were in a black dress, going to the theatre with Emilia List; it was during our separation. I know you will not have forgotten; it is vivid with me. Another time you were walking in the Thomasgasschen with an umbrella up, and you avoided me in desperation. And yet another time, as you were putting on your hat after a concert, our eyes happened to meet, and yours were full of the old unchanging love.

I picture you in all sorts of ways, as I have seen you since. I did not look at you much, but you charmed me so immeasurably… Ah, I can never praise you enough for yourself or for your love of me, which I don't really deserve.

Robert

Old love letters are best remembered

Gustave Flaubert to Louise Colet

Gustave Flaubert was a highly influential French novelist known for his perfection with words. He once wrote: 'Love is a springtime plant that perfumes everything with its hope, even the ruins to which it clings.'

(15 August 1846)

I will cover you with love when next I see you, with caresses, with ecstasy.

I want to gorge you with all the joys of the flesh, so that you faint and die.

I want you to be amazed by me, and to confess to yourself that you had never even dreamed of such transports.

I am the one who has been happy, now I want you to be the same.

When you are old, I want you to recall those few hours, I want your dry bones to quiver with joy when you think of them.

Old love letters are best remembered

34

Mark Twain to Olivia Langdon

Samuel Langhorne Clemens wrote under the pen name 'Mark Twain.' He was also a publisher, lecturer, humorist and entrepreneur. He became famous as the 'greatest humorist the United States has produced' and the 'Father of American Literature.' An asteroid discovered on 24 September 1976 was named '2632 Mark Twain' in his honour. He once said: 'Love seems the swiftest, but it is the slowest of all growths.'

Even if you prove to me that you have the blemishes you think you have, it cannot appall me any, because with them, you will still be better, and nobler, and lovelier than anyone I have known.

I will help you to weed out your faults when they are revealed to me but don't you be troubled about the matter, for you have a harder task before you, which is helping me to weed out mine.

Let me pay my due homage to your worth; let me honor you above all others; let me love you with a love that knows no doubt, no question—for you are my world, my life, my pride, my all of earth that is worth the having.

Let us hope and believe that we shall walk hand in hand down the lengthening highway of life, one in heart, one in impulse, and one in love, bearing each other's burdens, sharing each other's joys, soothing each other's griefs.

What we will lose of youth, we will make up in love, so that the account is squared, and to nobody's disadvantage.

I love you, my darling, and this my love will increase, step by step as tooth by tooth falls out, mile-stoning my way down to the great mystery and the Sweet Bye & Bye.

For I do love you…as the dew loves the flowers; as the birds love the sunshine; as the wavelets love the breeze, as mothers love their first-born; as memory loves old faces; as the yearning tides love the moon; as the angels love the pure in heart…

Take my kiss and my benediction, and try to be reconciled to the fact that I am

Yours forever,
Sam

Old love letters are best remembered

35

Pierre Curie to Marie Curie

Pierre Curie was a French physicist and one of the founding fathers of modern physics. He won the Nobel Prize in Physics in 1903 along with this wife Marie Curie.

He once said: 'Nothing in life is to be feared: it is only to be understood.'

(10 August 1894)

Nothing could have given me greater pleasure than to get news of you. The prospect of remaining two months without hearing about you had been extremely disagreeable to me: that is to say, your little note was more than welcome.

I hope you are laying up a stock of good air and that you will come back to us in October. As for me, I think I shall not go anywhere; I shall stay in the country, where I spend the whole day in front of my open window or in the garden.

We have promised each other—haven't we?—to be at least great friends. If you will only not change your mind! For there are no promises that are binding; such things cannot be ordered at will. It would be a fine thing, just the same, in which I hardly dare believe, to pass our lives near each other, hypnotized by our dreams: your patriotic dream, our humanitarian dream, and our scientific dream.

Of all those dreams the last is, I believe, the only legitimate one. I mean by that that we are powerless to change the social order and, even if we were not, we should not know what to do; in taking action, no matter in what direction, we should never be sure of not doing more harm than good, by retarding some inevitable evolution. From the scientific point of view, on the contrary, we may hope to do something; the ground is solider here, and any discovery that we may make, however small, will remain acquired knowledge.

See how it works out: it is agreed that we shall be great friends, but if you leave France in a year it would be an altogether too Platonic friendship, that of two creatures who would never see each other again. Wouldn't it be better for you to stay with me? I know that this question angers you, and that you don't want to speak of it again—and then, too, I feel so thoroughly unworthy of you from every point of view.

I thought of asking your permission to meet you by chance in Fribourg. But you are staying there, unless I am mistaken, only one day, and on that day you will of course belong to our friends the Kovalskis.

Believe me your very devoted
Pierre Curie

Old love letters are best remembered

G.K. Chesterton to Frances Blogg

G.K. Chesterton was a phenomenally prolific English writer, art and literary critic, and a philosopher. He is known as the 'Prince of Paradox.' He once wrote: 'Love is not blind; that is the last thing it is. Love is bound; and the more it is bound, the less it is blind.'

(1899)

Little as you may suppose it at the first glance, I have discovered that my existence until today has been, in truth, passed in the most intense gloom. Comparatively speaking, Pain, Hatred, Despair and Madness have been the companions of my days and nights. Nothing could woo a smile from my sombre and forbidding visage. Such (comparatively speaking) had been my previous condition. Intrinsically speaking it has been very jolly. But I never knew what being happy meant before tonight. Happiness is not at all smug: it is not peaceful or contented, as I have always been until today. Happiness brings not peace but a sword; it shakes you like rattling dice; it breaks your speech and darkens your sight. Happiness is stronger than oneself and sets its palpable foot upon one's neck.

Old love letters are best remembered

37

Allen Ginsberg to Peter Orlovsky

Allen Ginsberg was a well-known American writer and poet. He once wrote:

> *The weight of the world*
> *is love.*
> *Under the burden*
> *of solitude,*
> *under the burden*
> *of dissatisfaction*
>
> *the weight,*
> *the weight we carry*
> *is love.*

(20 January 1958)

Dear Petey:

O Heart O Love everything is suddenly turned to gold! Don't be afraid don't worry the most astounding beautiful thing has happened here! I don't know where to begin but the most important. When Bill came I, we, thought it was the same old Bill mad, but something had happened to Bill in the meantime since we last saw him...but last night finally Bill and I sat down facing each other across the kitchen table and looked eye to eye and talked, and I confessed all my doubt and misery—and in front of my eyes he turned into an Angel!

What happened to him in Tangiers this last few months? It seems he stopped writing and sat on his bed all afternoons thinking and meditating alone & stopped drinking—and finally dawned on his consciousness, slowly and repeatedly, every day, for several months—awareness of 'a benevolent sentient (feeling) center to the whole Creation'—he had apparently, in his own way, what I have been so hung up in myself and you, a vision of big peaceful Lovebrain—said it gave him (came sort of like a revelation slowly) courage to look at his whole life, me, him more dispassionately... We talked a long time got into tremendous rapport, very delicate, I almost trembled, a rapport much like yours and mine, but not sexual, he even began to dig my feelings about that, my willingness but really I don't want to, has stopped entirely putting pressure on me for bed—the whole nightmare's cleared up overnight, I woke this morning with great bliss of freedom & joy in my heart, Bill's saved, I'm saved, you're saved, we're all saved, everything has been all rapturous ever since—I only feel sad that perhaps you left as worried when we waved goodby and kissed so awkwardly—I wish I could have that over to say goodby to you happier & without the worries and doubts I had that dusty dusk when you left...— Bill is changed nature, I even feel much changed, great clouds rolled away, as I feel when you and I were in rapport, well, our rapport has remained in me, with me, rather than losing it, I'm feeling to everyone, something of the same as between us. And you? What's happening inside Dear Pete? I read Bill your poems, I'll type them & send them soon, everything is happening so fast. I feel like I can write even. Are you OK? Write me happy letter, don't be sad, I love you, nothing can change love, beautiful love, once we have it…

Old love letters are best remembered

38

Michael Faraday to Sarah Barnard

This is an apologia pro vita sua from a man of science who is so engrossed in the jargon and terminology of science that he finds it difficult to fully confess his feelings and love. However, the undercurrent is obvious!

(Royal Institution, Thursday evening, December 1820)

My dear Sarah—

It is astonishing how much the state of the body influences the powers of the mind. I have been thinking all the morning of the very delightful and interesting letter I would send you this evening, and now I am so tired, and yet have so much to do, that my thoughts are quite giddy, and run round your image without any power of themselves to stop and admire it.

I want to say a thousand kind and, believe me, heart-felt things to you, but am not master of words fit for the purpose; and still, as I ponder and think on you, chlorides, trials, oil, Davy, steel, miscellanea, mercury, and fifty other professional fancies swim before and drive me further and further into the quandary of stupidness.

From your affectionate
Michael

Old love letters are best remembered

39

Jean-Paul Sartre to Simone de Beauvoir

Jean-Paul Sartre was a French novelist, playwright, screenwriter, literary critic, biographer and political activist. He won the Nobel Prize in Literature on 22 October 1964, which he declined, as he did not want to be 'turned into an institution'.

Sartre believed that one could experience the joy of love when one achieved security and meaning through one's relationships with other people.

(1926)

My dear little girl

For a long time I've been wanting to write to you in the evening after one of those outings with friends that I will soon be describing in 'A Defeat,' the kind when the world is ours. I wanted to bring you my conqueror's joy and lay it at your feet, as they did in the Age of the Sun King. And then, tired out by all the shouting, I always simply went to bed. Today I'm doing it to feel the pleasure you don't yet know, of turning abruptly from friendship to love, from strength to tenderness. Tonight I love you in a way that you have not known in me: I am neither worn down by travels nor wrapped up in the desire for your presence. I am mastering my love for you and turning it inwards as a constituent element of myself. This happens much more often than I admit to you, but seldom when I'm writing to you. Try to understand me: I love you while paying attention to external things. At Toulouse I simply loved you. Tonight I love you on a spring evening. I love you with the window open. You are mine, and things are mine, and my love alters the things around me and the things around me alter my love.

My dear little girl, as I've told you, what you're lacking is friendship. But now is the time for more practical advice. Couldn't you find a woman friend? How can Toulouse fail to contain one intelligent young woman worthy of you? But you wouldn't have to love her. Alas, you're always ready to give your love, it's the easiest thing to get from you. I'm not talking about your love for me, which is well beyond that, but you are lavish with little secondary loves, like that night in Thiviers when you loved that peasant walking downhill in the dark, whistling away, who turned out to be me. Get to know the feeling, free of tenderness, that comes from being two. It's hard, because all friendship, even between two red-blooded men, has its moments of love. I have only to console my grieving friend to love him; it's a feeling easily weakened and distorted. But you're capable of it, and you must experience it. And so, despite your fleeting misanthropy, have you imagined what a lovely adventure it would be to search Toulouse for a woman who would be worthy of you and whom you wouldn't be in love with? Don't bother with the physical side or the social situation. And search honestly. And if you find nothing, turn Henri Pons, whom you scarcely love anymore, into a friend.

[...]
I love you with all my heart and soul.

Old love letters are best remembered

40

Thomas Otway to Elizabeth Barry

Thomas Otway was an English dramatist of the Restoration Period. He died at the young age of 33 years. He wrote once: 'If we must part forever, give me but one kind word to think upon and please myself with, while my heart's breaking.'

∿

(c. 1677–78)

Could I see you without passion, or be absent from you without pain, I need not beg your pardon for thus renewing my vows that I love you more than health, or any happiness here or hereafter.

Everything you do is a new charm to me, and though I have languished for seven long tedious years of desire, jealously despairing, yet every minute I see you I still discover something new and more bewitching.

Consider how I love you; what would I not renounce or enterprise for you?

I must have you mine, or I am miserable, and nothing but knowing which shall be the happy hour can make the rest of my years that are to come tolerable. Give me a word or two of comfort, or resolve never to look on me more, for I cannot bear a kind look and after it a cruel denial.

This minute my heart aches for you; and, if I cannot have a right in yours, I wish it would ache till I could complain to you no longer. Remember poor

Otway

Old love letters are best remembered

41

Winston Churchill to Clementine Churchill

The oddities of love letters: the Churchills signed off their love letters with rudimentary drawings of animals, based on the nicknames they called each other—Winston was 'pug', and Clementine was 'cat'. In this letter, which Winston sent to Clementine from Germany a year after they got married, he drew a 'galloping pug—for European travel' on the last page. 'P.K.' here refers to their eldest daughter, affectionately nicknamed 'puppy kitten'.

(Kronprinz Hotel, Wurzburg, 15 September 1909)

My darling, We have been out all day watching these great manoeuvres...

 I have a very nice horse from the Emperor's stable, & am able to ride about wherever I chose with a suitable retinue. As I am supposed to be an 'Excellency' I get a vy good place. Freddie on the other hand is ill-used. These people are so amazingly routine that anything the least out of the ordinary—anything they have not considered officially & for months—upsets them dreadfully... I saw the Emperor today & had a few mintues' talk with him. He is vy sallow—but otherwise looks quite well…

We have had a banquet tonight at the Bavarian palace. A crowd of princes & princelets & the foreign officers of various countries. It began at 6 p.m. & was extremely dull…

This army is a terrible engine. It marches sometimes 35 miles in a day. It is in number as the sands of the sea—& with all the modern conveniences. There is a complete divorce between the two sides of German life—the Imperialists & Socialist. Nothing unites them. They are two different nations. With us there are so many shades. Here it is all black & white (the Prussian colours). I think another 50 years will see a wiser & gentler world. But we shall not be spectators of it. Only the P.K. will glitter in a happier scene. How easily men could make things much better than they are—if only all tried together! Much as was attracts me & fascinates my mind with its tremendous situation—I feel more deeply every year—& can measure the feeling here in the midst of arms—what vile & wicked folly & barbarism it all is.

Sweet cat—I kiss your vision as it rises before my mind. Your dear heart throbs often in my own. God bless you darling keep you safe & sound.

Kiss the P.K. for me all over

With fondest love
W.

Old love letters are best remembered

42

Juliette Drouet to Victor Hugo

Juliette Drouet was a French actress who quit her career after she became the mistress of Victor Hugo. Victor Hugo once said:

> *'Love is like a tree. It grows by itself, roots itself deeply in our being and continues to flourish over a heart in ruin.'*
>
> *'Life is the flower for which love is the honey.'*

(1835, Friday, 8 p.m.)

If I were a clever woman, my gorgeous bird, I could describe to you how you unite in yourself the beauties of form, plumage, and song! I would tell you that you are the greatest marvel of all ages, and I should only be speaking the simple truth. But to put all this into suitable words, my superb one, I should require a voice far more harmonious than that which is bestowed upon my species—for I am the humble owl that you mocked at only lately. Therefore, it cannot be. I will not tell you to what degree you are dazzling and resplendent. I leave that to the birds of sweet song who, as you know, are none the less beautiful and appreciative.

I am content to delegate to them the duty of watching, listening and admiring, while to myself I reserve the right of loving; this may be less attractive to the ear, but it is sweeter far to the heart. I love you, I love you, my Victor; I cannot reiterate it too often; I can never express it as much as I feel it.

I recognise *you* in all the beauty that surrounds me—in form, in colour, in perfume, in harmonious sound: all of these mean *you* to me. You are superior to them all. You are not only the solar spectrum with the seven luminous colours, but the sun himself, that illumines, warms, and revivifies the whole world! That is what you are, and I am the lowly woman who adores you.

Juliette.

If you are coming to fetch me, as you led me to expect, I shall see you very soon now. I have never longed more ardently for you. Lanvin has just come. I will tell you about it when I see you.

Old love letters are best remembered

43

Edgar Allan Poe to Annie L. Richmond

While he was lecturing in Lowell, Massachusetts, Edgar Allan Poe met Nancy Richmond, the wife of a paper manufacturer, in July 1848. Although they were both attracted to each other, their relationship never became romantic. Poe referred to Richmond as 'Annie' and wrote her the poem 'For Annie'. She legally changed her name to Annie 20 years after Poe's death.

(Fordham, 16 November 1848)

Ah, Annie Annie! my Annie! what cruel thoughts about your Eddy must have been torturing your heart during the last terrible fortnight, in which you have heard nothing from me—not even one little word to say that I still lived & loved you. But Annie I know that you felt too deeply the nature of my love for you, to doubt that, even for one moment, & this thought has comforted me in my bitter sorrow—I could bear that you should imagine every other evil except that one—that my soul had been untrue to yours. Why am I not with you now darling that I might sit by your side, press your dear hand in mine, & look deep down into the clear Heaven of your eyes—so that the words which I now can only write, might sink into your heart, and make you comprehend what it is that I would say—And yet Annie, all that I wish to say—all that my soul pines to express at this instant, is included in the one word, love—To be with you now—so that I might whisper in your ear the divine emotion[s], which agitate me—I would willingly—oh joyfully abandon this world with all my hopes of another:—but you believe this, Annie—you do believe it, & will always believe it—So long as I think that you know I love you, as no man ever loved woman—so long as I think you comprehend in some measure, the fervor with which I adore you, so long, no worldly trouble can ever render me absolutely wretched. But oh, my darling, my Annie, my own sweet sister Annie, my pure beautiful angel—wife of my soul—to be mine hereafter & forever in the Heavens—how shall I explain to you the bitter, bitter anguish which has tortured me since I left you? You saw, you felt the agony of grief with which I bade you farewell—You remember my expressions of gloom—of a dreadful horrible foreboding of ill—Indeed—indeed it seemed to me that death approached me even then, & that I was involved in the shadow which went before him—As I clasped you to my heart, I said to myself—'it is for the last time, until we meet in Heaven'—I remember nothing distinctly, from that moment until I found myself in Providence—I went to bed & wept through a long, long, hideous night of despair—When the day broke, I arose & endeavored to quiet my mind by a rapid walk in the cold, keen air—but all would not do—the demon tormented me still. Finally I procured two ounces of laudnum & without returning to my Hotel, took the cars back to Boston. When I arrived, I wrote you a letter, in which I opened my whole heart to you—to you—my Annie, whom I so madly, so distractedly love—I told you how my struggles were more than I could bear—how my soul revolted from saying the words which were to be said—and that not even for your dear sake, could I bring myself to say them. I then reminded you of that holy promise, which was the last I exacted from you in parting—the promise that, under all circumstances, you would come to me on my bet of death—I implored you to come then—mentioning the place where I should be found in Boston—Having written this letter, I swallowed about half the laudnum & hurried to the Post-Office—intending not to take the rest until I saw you—for, I did not doubt for one moment, that my own Annie would keep her sacred promise—But I had not calculated on the strength of the laudanum, for, before I reached the Post Office my reason was entirely gone, & the letter was never put in. Let me pass over, my darling Sister, the awful horrors which succeeded—A friend was at hand, who aided & (if it can be called saving) saved me—but it is only within the last three days that I have been able to remember what occurred in that dreary interval—It appears that, after the laudanum was rejected from the stomach, I became calm, & to a casual observer, sane—so that I was suffered to go back to Providence—Here I saw her, & spoke, for your sake, the words which you urged me to speak—Ah Annie Annie! my Annie!—is your heart so strong?—is there no hope!—is there none?—I feel that I must die if I persist, & yet, how can I now retract with honor?—Ah beloved, think—think for me & for yourself—do I not love you Annie? do you not love me? Is not this all? Beyond this blissful thought, what other consideration can there be in this dreary world! It is not much that I ask, sweet sister Annie—my mother & myself would take a small cottage at Westford—oh so small—so very humble—I should be far away from the tumult[s] of the world—from the ambition which I loathe—I would labor day & night, and with industry, I could accomplish so much—Annie! it would be a Paradise beyond my wildest hopes—I could see some of your beloved family every day, & you often—oh VERY often—I would hear from you continually—regularly & our dear mother would be with us & love us both—ah darling—do not these pictures touch your inmost heart? Think—oh think for me—before the words—the vows are spoken, which put yet another terrible bar between us—before the time goes by, beyond which there must be no thinking—I call upon you in the name of God—in the name of the holy love I bear you, to be sincere with me—Can you, my Annie, bear to think I am another's? It would give me supreme—infinite bliss to hear you say that you could not bear it—I am at home now with my dear muddle who is endeavoring to comfort me—but the sole words which soothe me, are those in which she speaks of 'my Annie'—she tells me that she has written you, begging you to come on to Fordham—ah beloved Annie, IS IT NOT POSSIBLE? I am so ill—so terribly, hopelessly ILL in body and mind, that I feel I CANNOT live, unless I can feel your sweet, gentle, loving hand pressed upon my forehead—oh my pure, virtuous, generous, beautiful, beautiful sister Annie!—is it not POSSIBLE for you to come—if only for one little week?—until I subdue this fearful agitation, which if continued, will either destroy my life or, drive me hopelessly mad—Farewell—here & hereafter—

forever your own
Eddy—

Old love letters are best remembered

44

George Washington to Sarah Cary Fairfax

George Washington married Martha Custis in 1759, and was faithful to her throughout the forty years of their marriage, until his death in 1799. However, evidence indicates that he had held a torch for another woman before his marriage to Martha, and possibly continued to afterwards—a woman named Sarah Cary 'Sally' Fairfax, the wife of Washington's friend George William Fairfax.

(Camp at Fort Cumberland, 12 September 1758)

Dear Madam,

Yesterday I was honourd with your short, but very agreable favour of the first Instt. how joyfully I catch at the happy occasion of renewing a Corrispondance which I feard was disrelishd on your part, I leave to time, that never failing Expositor of All things.—and to a Monitor equally as faithful in my own Breast, to Testifie. In silence I now express my Joy.—Silence which in some cases—I wish the present— speaks more Intelligably than the sweetest Eloquence.

If you allow that any honour can be derivd from my

opposition to Our present System of management, you destroy the merit of it entirely in me by attributing my anxiety to the annimating prospect of possessing Mrs Custis. When—I—need not name it.—guess yourself.—Shoud not my own Honour, and Country's welfare be the excitement? Tis true, I profess myself a Votary to Love—I acknowledge that a Lady is in the Case—and further I confess, that this Lady is known to you.—Yes Madam, as well as she is to one, who is too sensible of her Charms to deny the Power, whose Influence he feels and must ever Submit to. I feel the force of her amiable beauties in the recollection of a thousand tender passages that I coud wish to obliterate, till I am bid to revive them.—but experience alas! sadly reminds me how Impossible this is.—and evinces an Opinion which I have long entertaind, that there is a Destiny, which has the Sovereign controul of our Actions—not to be resisted by the strongest efforts of Human Nature.

You have drawn me my dear Madam, or rather have I drawn myself, into an honest confession of a Simple Fact—misconstrue not my meaning—'tis obvious—doubt it not, nor expose it,—the World has no business to know the object of my Love, declard in this manner to—you when I want to conceal it—One thing, above all things in this World I wish to know, and only one person of your Acquaintance can solve me that, or guess my meaning.—but adieu to this, till happier times, if I ever shall see them.—the hours at present are melancholy dull.—neither the rugged Toils of War, nor the gentler conflict of A——B—s is in my choice.—I dare believe you are as happy as you say—I wish I was happy also—Mirth, good Humour, ease of Mind and.—what else? cannot fail to render you so; and consummate your Wishes.

If one agreable Lady coud almost wish herself a fine Gentleman for the sake of another; I apprehend, that many fine Gentlemen will wish themselves finer, e'er Mrs Spotswood is possest.—She has already become a reigning Toast in this Camp; and many there are in it, who intends—(fortune favouring)—to make honourable Scar's speak the fulness of their Merit, and be a messenger of their Love to Her.

I cannot easily forgive the unseasonable haste of my last Express, if he deprivd me thereby of a single word you intended to add.—the time of the present messenger is, as the last might have been, entirely at your disposal.—I cant expect to hear from my Friends more than this once, before the Fate of the Expedition will, some how or other be determind, I therefore beg to know when you set out for Hampton; & when you expect to Return to Belvoir again—and I shoud be glad to hear also of your speedy departure, as I shall thereby hope for your return before I get down; the disappointment of seeing your Family woud give me much concern.—From any thing I can yet see 'tis hardly possible to say when we shall finish—I dont think there is a probability of it till the middle of November. Your Letter to Captn Gist I forwarded by a safe hand the moment it came to me.—his answer shall be carefully transmitted.

Colo. Mercer to whom I deliverd your message and Compliments, Joins me very heartily in wishing you and the Ladies of Belvoir the perfect enjoyment of every Happiness this World affords.—be assured that I am Dr Madam with the most unfeigned regard, Yr Most Obedient & Most Obligd Hble Servt

Go: Washington

Old love letters are best remembered

45

Mary Wollstonecraft to William Godwin

Mary Wollstonecraft was a British writer and philosopher and an advocate of women's rights.

(4 October 1796)

I would have liked to have dined with you today, after finishing your essay—that my eyes, and lips, I do not exactly mean my voice, might have told you that they had raised you in my esteem. What a cold word! I would say love, if you will promise not to dispute about its propriety, when I want to express an increasing affection, founded on a more intimate acquaintance with your heart and understanding.

I shall cork up all my kindness—yet the fine volatile essence may fly off in my walk—you know not how much tenderness for you may escape in a voluptuous sigh, should the air, as is often the case, give a pleasurable movement to the sensations, that have been clustering round my heart, as I read this morning—reminding myself, every now and then, that the writer loved me.

Voluptuous is often expressive of a meaning I do not now intend to give, I would describe one of those moments, when the senses are exactly tuned by the ringing tenderness of the heart and according reason entices you to live in the present moment, regardless of the past or future—it is not rapture—it is sublime tranquility.

I have felt it in your arms—hush! Let not the light see, I was going to say hear it—these confessions should only be uttered—you know where, when the curtains are up—and all the world shut out—Ah me!

I wish I may find you at home when I carry this letter to drop it in the box,—that I may drop a kiss with it into your heart, to be embalmed, till me meet, closer.

Old love letters are best remembered

46

Isadora Duncan to Gordon Craig

American-born Isadora Duncan's star was rising in Europe at the turn of the twentieth century. She scripted history as one of the creators of modern dance and drew large crowds to her contemporary dance performances.

At one such performance in Berlin in 1904, Gordon Craig, theatre designer and son of famous actress Ellen Terry, saw Isadora for the first time. According to his own admission, he felt speechless, utterly awed—mesmerized by her 'primal and ethereal' movements. After the performance ended, he went to meet her in her dressing room. Cupid struck! She was just as attracted to Craig, and asked him out to dinner.

(Grand Hotel D'Europe, St Petersburg, Rue Michel, 25 December 1904)

Just arrived this morning—Christmas morning

Here it's the 12 of December (remember the 12 days of Christmas)

My Darling—

I don't like it at all. All the Chairs are staring at me in the most frightful way—And there is a Lady on the Mantel piece who has taken a Great objection to me—and I'm awfully scared—

This is no place for a person with a nice cheerful disposition like me—it looks like those parlors in the Novels where they plot things—

All night long the train has not been flying over but going pim de pim over Great fields of snow—vast plains of snow—Great bare Countries covered with snow (Walt Whitman could have written 'em up fine) and over all this the Moon shining—and across the window always a Golden shower of sparks—from the locomotive—it was quite worth seeing and I lay there looking out on it all and thinking of you—of you, you dearest sweetest best darling—

The City is covered in snow and little sleighs rushing madly about—All things go in sliders of course. I send you many little missives along the way—Hope they arrived!—

I must go now and wash the soot off and have my Breakfast.

[…]

Give my love to Dear Dear No. 11 and to that musty little dear Home No. 6 and for your dear self my heart is overflowing with just the most unoriginal old fashionest sort of love.

Write to me—and tell me—I go now to splash
Your Isadora

Old love letters are best remembered

Tsarina Alexandra to Tsar Nicholas II of Russia

Tsarina Alexandra was the last empress of Russia during the reign of her husband Emperor Nicholas II. She once said: 'Fill your days with love...'

(30 December 1915)

Off you go again alone and it's with a very heavy heart I part from you. No more kisses and tender caresses for ever so long—I want to bury myself in you, hold you tight in my arms, make you feel the intense love of mine.

You are my very life Sweetheart, and every separation gives such endless heartache...

Goodbye my Angel, Husband of my heart I envy my flowers that will accompany you. I press you tightly to my breast, kiss every sweet place with tender love...

God bless and protect you, guard you from all harm, guide you safely and firmly into the new year. May it bring glory and sure peace, and the reward for all this war has cost you.

I gently press my lips to yours and try to forget everything, gazing into your lovely eyes—I lay on your precious breast, rested my tired head upon it still. This morning I tried to gain calm and strength for the separation.

Goodbye wee one, Lovebird, Sunshine, Huzy mine, Own!

Old love letters are best remembered

Charlie Parker to Chan Parker

Charlie Parker was an American Jazz saxophonist, composer and band leader. His nickname was 'Yardbird' or 'Bird.' He played an influential role in creating pop saxophone music. As Aberjhani once wrote about jazz music: 'At the edge of madness you howl diamonds and pearls.'

To you;

The way I thought was wrong, having not known, it was right. Here is the proof of my feelings, Don't hate me, love me forever:—

Beautiful is the world, slow is one to take advantage. Wind up the world the other way. And at the start of the turning of the earth, lie my feelings for thou.

To you
Shame on me.
I love you.

Old love letters are best remembered

49

Radclyffe Hall to Evguenia Souline

Here comes a letter written by the English writer Radclyffe Hall to Evguenia Souline, a Russian émigré. Hall is best known for her 1928 novel The Well of Loneliness. *She broke conventions by deciding to go by the masculine name of 'John' instead of her given name, Marguerite, and by writing openly about her lesbian identity.*

(24 October 1934)

Why is it that the people I write of are so very often lonely people? Are they? I think that perhaps you may be right. I greatly feel the loneliness of the soul—nearly every soul is more or less lonely. Then again: I have been called the writer of 'misfits.' And it may be that being myself a 'misfit,' for as you know, beloved, I am a born invert, it may be that I am a writer of 'misfits' in one form or another—I think I understand them—their joys & their sorrows, indeed I know I do, and all the misfits of this world are lonely, being conscious that they differ from the rank and file. When we meet you & I will talk of my work and you shall be my critic, my darling. If you wish to you shall be very rude—but I do hope you like your John's work just a little. I want you to like my work, Soulina.

Darling—I wonder if you realize how much I am counting on your coming to England, how much it means to me—it means all the world, and indeed my body shall be all, all yours, as yours will be all, all mine, beloved. And we two will lie close in each others arms, close, close, always trying to lie even closer, and I will kiss your mouth and your eyes and your breasts—I will kiss your body all over—And you shall kiss me back again many times as you kissed me when we were in Paris. And nothing will matter but just we two, we two longing loves at last come together. I wake up in the night & think of these things & then I can't sleep for my longing, Soulina. This is love—make no mistake about it—love has come to you—you are loved and loved. No one whom you meet is more loved than you are—no one in the whole world can be more loved. When you look at people you can say to yourself in your heart—'I also has (sic) got a lover—I am loved until the love is as pain, as a scourge of whips on my lover's back, as a fire that torments and consumes my lover.' Blessed is this lover that torments day and night, night & day, for it also illumines and sustains when the loved one is kind—be kind, then, my Soulina.

Your John

Old love letters are best remembered

50

Violet Trefusis to Vita Sackville-West

Violet Trefusis was a British author and socialite. She once said: 'I love belonging to you—I glory in it.'

(22 July 1918)

… For 16 nights I have listened expectantly for the opening of my door, for the whispered 'Lushka' as you entered my room, and tonight I am alone. What shall I do? How can I sleep?…I don't want to sleep, for fear of waking up, thinking you near by my side, and stretching out my arms to clasp—emptiness!
  Mitya, do you remember this?

> All that I know of love I learned of you,
> And I know all that lovers can know,
> Since passionately loving to be loved
> The subtlety of your wise body moved
> My senses to a curiosity
> And your wise heart adorned itself for me.
> Did you not teach me how to love you, how
> To win you, how to suffer for you now
> Since you have made, as long as life endures,
> My very nerves, my very senses, yours?
> I suffer for you now with that same skill

Of self-consuming ecstasy, whose thrill
(May Death some day the thought of it remove!)
You gathered form the very hands of Love.

… I think you now do realize that this can't go on, that we must once and for all take our courage in both hands, and go away together. What sort of a life can we lead now? Yours, an infamous and degrading lie to the world, officially bound to someone you don't care for, perpetually with that someone, that in itself constitutes an outrage to me, being constantly watched and questioned, watched to see if the expected reaction is not taking place, questioned to make quite sure there is no one else!

I, not caring a damn for anyone but you, utterly lost, miserably incomplete, condemned to leading a futile, purposeless existence, which no longer holds the smallest attraction for me…

A cheery picture, isn't it? And you know how true it is. At all events, I implore you to run the H.N. fiction to death. It is the only thing that can save us, the only thing that will ensure peace for both of us.

En attendant, I think 'there is a lot to be said for being (temporarily) dead'. Mitya, what stabs me like a knife is to remember you here in this room watching the last things being packed preparatory to going away with you, a fortnight ago. When I think of that and you waiting for me on the stairs, I feel quite faint from the pain of it all. My God, how exultant we were! And now, 'la vie est devenue cendre dans son fruit'. There is nothing to look forward to, nothing.

I never thought I would (or could) love like this….

Old love letters are best remembered

51

Love Letters in William Shakespeare's Plays

Shakespeare was an English poet, actor and playwright, regarded as the greatest writer in the English language. He is known as National Poet of England. He is the first person other than royalty to be portrayed on the British stamp.

He famously stated: 'If music be the food of love, play on.'

From *As You Like It*: Orland to Rosalind

> From the east to western Ind
> No jewel is like Rosalind.
> Her worth being mounted on the wind,
> Through all the world bears Rosalind.
> All the pictures fairest lined
> Are but black to Rosalind.
> Let no face be kept in mind
> But the fair of Rosalind. (3.2.88–95)

From *Hamlet*: Hamlet to Ophelia

> To the celestial, and my soul's idol, the most
> beautified Ophelia—
> [...]
> In her excellent white bosom, these, etc.—
> [...]
>
> Doubt thou the stars are fire,
> Doubt that the sun doth move,
> Doubt truth to be a liar,
> But never doubt I love.
>
> O dear Ophelia, I am ill at these numbers. I have not
> art to reckon my groans, but that I love thee best, O
> most best, believe it. Adieu.
> Thine evermore, most dear lady, whilst
> this machine is to him, Hamlet. (2.2)

From *The Two Gentlemen of Verona*: Proteus to Julia

> O hateful hands, to tear such loving words!
> Injurious wasps, to feed on such sweet honey
> And kill the bees that yield it with your stings!
> I'll kiss each several paper for amends.
> [She picks up some pieces.]
> Look, here is writ 'kind Julia.' Unkind Julia,
> As in revenge of thy ingratitude,
> I throw thy name against the bruising stones,
> Trampling contemptuously on thy disdain.
> And here is writ 'love-wounded Proteus.'

Poor wounded name, my bosom as a bed
Shall lodge thee till thy wound be thoroughly healed,
And thus I search it with a sovereign kiss.
But twice or thrice was 'Proteus' written down.
Be calm, good wind. Blow not a word away
Till I have found each letter in the letter
Except mine own name. That some whirlwind bear
Unto a ragged, fearful, hanging rock
And throw it thence into the raging sea.
Lo, here in one line is his name twice writ:
'Poor forlorn Proteus, passionate Proteus,
To the sweet Julia.' That I'll tear away—
And yet I will not, sith so prettily
He couples it to his complaining names. (1.2.112–134)

Old love letters are best remembered

52

Esther Vanhomrigh to Jonathan Swift

Esther Vanhomrigh was an Irish woman who corresponded with Jonathan Swift for a long time. Swift once said: 'Bachelor's fare: Bread, cheese, and kisses.'

(Celbridge, 1720)

Believe me t'is with the utmost regret that I now complain to you, because I know your good nature such, that you cannot see any humaine creature miserable, without being sensibly touched yett what can I do I must either unload my heart and tell you all its griefs or sink under the unexpressable distress I now suffer by your prodigious neglect of me. T'is now ten long weeks since I saw you and in all that time I have never received but one letter from you, and a little note with an excuse. Oh—how have you forgott me you indeavour by severities to force me from you nor can I blame you for with the utmost distress and confusion I behold my self the cause of uneasy reflections to you yet I cannot comfo[rt] you; but here declair that t'is not in the power of arte time or accedent to lessen the unexpressable passion which I have for—put my passion under the utmost restraint send me as distant from you as the earth will alow yet you can not banish those charming Idaea's which will ever stick by me while I have the use of memory nor is the love I beare you only seated in my soul for there is not a single atome of my frame that is not blended with it therefor don't flatter your self that separation will ever change my sentiments for I find my self unquiat in the midst of silence and my heart is at once pierced with sorrow and love for heavens sake tell me what has caused this prodigious change in you which I have found of late If you have the least remains of pitty for me left tell it me tenderly no don't tell it so that it may cause my present Death and don't suffer me to live a life like a languishing Death which is the only life I can leade if you have lost any of your tenderness for me.

Old love letters are best remembered

53

Abigail Adams to John Adams

Abigail Adams, an extraordinary, diplomatic woman, was the wife of John Adams. She was also his closest advisor. Both wrote more than 1,000 letters to each other in their lifetimes.

John Adams once said: 'I am, as I ever was and ever shall be, yours, yours, yours...'

(Weymouth, 11 August 1763)

My Friend

If I was sure your absence to day was occasioned, by what it generally is, either to wait upon Company, or promote some good work, I freely confess my Mind would be much more at ease than at present it is. Yet this uneasiness does not arise from any apprehension of Slight or neglect, but a fear least you are indisposed, for that you said should be your only hindrance.

Humanity obliges us to be affected with the distresses and Miserys of our fellow creatures. Friendship is a band yet stronger, which causes us to [fee]l with greater tenderness the afflictions of our Friends.

And there is a tye more binding than Humanity, and stronger than Friendship, which makes us anxious for the happiness and welfare of those to whom it binds us. It makes their Misfortunes, Sorrows and afflictions, our own. Unite these, and there is a threefold cord—by this cord I am not ashamed to own myself bound, nor do I [believe] that you are wholly free from it. Judg[e you then] for your Diana has she not this day [had sufficien]t cause for pain and anxiety of mind?

She bids me [tell] you that Seneca, for the sake of his Paulina was careful and tender of his health. The health and happiness of Seneca she says was not dearer to his Paulina, than that of Lysander to his Diana.

The Fabrick often wants repairing and if we neglect it the Deity will not long inhabit it, yet after all our care and solisitude to preserve it, it is a tottering Building, and often reminds us that it will finally fall.

Adieu may this find you in better health than I fear it will, and happy as your Diana wishes you.

Accept this hasty Scrawl warm from the Heart of Your Sincere

Diana

(23 December 1782)

[...] should I draw you the picture of my heart it would be what I hope you would still love though it contained nothing new. The early possession you obtained there, and the absolute power you have obtained over it, leaves not the smallest space unoccupied.

I look back to the early days of our acquaintance and friendship as to the days of love and innocence, and, with an indescribable pleasure, I have seen near a score of years roll over our heads with an affection heightened and improved by time, nor have the dreary years of absence in the smallest degree effaced from my mind the image of the dear untitled man to whom I gave my heart.

[...]

Old love letters are best remembered

54

Emily Dickinson to Susan Gilbert

Emily Dickinson was an American poet who was not very well-known during her lifetime, but became a prominent literary figure in American poetry posthumously. She wrote about Susan Gilbert:

> To own a Susan of my own
> Is of itself a Bliss—
> Whatever realm I forfeit, Lord,
> Continue me in this.

∫

(Early spring, 1852)

Will you be kind to me, Susie? I am naughty and cross, this morning, and nobody loves me here; nor would you love me, if you should see me frown, and hear how loud the door bangs whenever I go through; and yet it isn't anger—I don't believe it is, for when nobody sees, I brush away big tears with the corner of my apron, and then go working on—bitter tears, Susie—so hot that they burn my cheeks, and almost scorch my eyeballs, but you have wept much, and you know they are less of anger than sorrow.

And I do love to run fast—and hide away from them all; here in dear Susie's bosom, I know is love and rest, and I never would go away, did not the big world call me, and beat me for not working... Your precious letter, Susie, it sits here now, and smiles so kindly at me, and gives me such sweet thoughts of the dear writer. When you come home, darling, I shan't have your letters, shall I, but I shall have yourself, which is more—Oh more, and better, than I can even think! I sit here with my little whip, cracking the time away, till not an hour is left of it—then you are here! And Joy is here—joy now and forevermore!

Old love letters are best remembered

55

Leigh Hunt to Marianne Kent Hunt

Leigh Hunt was an English poet, essayist and critic. Some of his thoughts on love are expressed in these quotes by him: 'Stolen kisses are always sweetest'; 'There are two worlds: the world we can measure with line and rule, and the world that we feel with our hearts and imagination.'

(Enfield, Friday, 14 October 1803, 3 o'clock)

My dear Marian, I arrived here last night about half past six in a very cold dew-fall, and am as well and as happy as the effects of yesterday's head-ache and absence from you will allow me to be. I thank God, that my head was at none of its tantrums last night; I have had but a slight pinch of it about five this morning, and trust that the fine exhilarating breezes from Enfield Chace and its beautiful hills covered with wood will sweep the tormentor from my temples entirely. Mr. M.was so occupied with his business yesterday afternoon that he could not leave town with me, and will not come down till six this evening, so that I am alone with his wife, a pretty lively woman of twenty seven: however, I advise you not to be uneasy; I eat my breakfast with quite as good an appetite as I do when alone, though the lady sits right opposite me, and assure you that out of twenty kisses, which my brother Robert commissioned me to give her from him, I have given not a single one:—after all it would be no matter either to you or me, if I discharged my commission in the best of a[ll] possible manners; I should feel as little in saluting Mrs. M. as in saluting a female statue, and often boast to myself of the real affection I cherish for you in the idea, that I could kiss all the beauties in the Grand Seignior's seraglio with as little emotion as a bunch of turnips, while I have only to touch your lips, and it sets me trembling like an aspin leaf.

Old love letters are best remembered

56

Mary Hutchinson Wordsworth to William Wordsworth

Mary Hutchinson Wordsworth was the wife of the leading English Romantic poet William Wordsworth. William once said: 'Write to me frequently and the longest letters possible; never mind whether you have facts or no to communicate; fill your paper with the breathings of your heart.'

(Grasmere, 1812)

O My William!

It is not in my power to tell thee how I have been affected by this dearest of all letters—it was so unexpected—so new a thing to see the breathing of thy inmost heart upon paper that I was quite overpowered, & now that I sit down to answer thee in the loneliness & depth of that love which unites us & which cannot be felt but by ourselves, I am so agitated & my eyes are so bedimmed that I scarcely know how to proceed—I have brought my paper, after having laid my baby upon thy sacred pillow, into my own, into THY own room—& write from Sara's little Table, retired from the window which looks upon the lasses strewing out the hay to an uncertain Sun.

Old love letters are best remembered

Claire Clairmont to Lord Byron

Clara Mary Jane Clairmont, known commonly as Claire Clairmont, was the stepsister of the famous writer Mary Shelley. A famous quote by Lord Byron goes: 'Love will find a way through paths where wolves fear to prey.'
He aptly expresses the intensity of the emotion of love in this excerpt from his poem 'When We Two Parted':

> *In secret we met—*
> *In silence I grieve,*
> *The heart could forget,*
> *The spirit deceive.*
> *If I should meet thee*
> *After long years,*
> *How should I greet thee?—*
> *With silence and tears.*

(1816)

You bid me write short to you and I have much to say. You also bade me believe that it was a fancy which made me cherish an attachment for you. It cannot be a fancy since you have been for the last year the object upon which every solitary moment led me to muse.

I do not expect you to love me, I am not worthy of your love. I feel you are superior, yet much to my surprise, more to my happiness, you betrayed passions I had believed no longer alive in your bosom. Shall I also have to ruefully experience the want of happiness? Shall I reject it when it is offered? I may appear to you imprudent, vicious; my opinions detestable, my theory depraved; but one thing, at least, time shall show you: that I love gently and with affection, that I am incapable of anything approaching to the feeling of revenge or malice; I do assure you, your future will shall be mine, and everything you shall do or say, I shall not question.

[...]

Old love letters are best remembered

58

John Ruskin to Effie Gray

John Ruskin was a famous English writer and a keen geologist. He once said, 'It is better to lose your pride with someone you love rather than to lose that someone you love with your useless pride.'

(December 1847)

I don't know anything dreadful enough to liken to you—you are like a sweet forest of pleasant glades and whispering branches—where people wander on and on in its playing shadows they know not how far—and when they come near the centre of it, it is all cold and impenetrable—and when they would fain turn, lo—they are hedged with briars and thorns and cannot escape…

You are like the bright—soft—swelling—lovely fields of a high glacier covered with fresh morning snow—which is heavenly to the eye—and soft and winning on the foot—but beneath, there are winding clefts and dark places in its cold—cold ice—where men fall, and rise not again.

Old love letters are best remembered

59

Edith Wharton to W. Morton Fullerton

Edith Wharton was an American novelist and an interior designer. She once stated: 'There is one friend in the life of each of us who seems not a separate person, however dear and beloved, but an expansion, an interpretation, of one's self the very meaning of one's soul.'

(26 August 1908)

Dear, won't you tell me the meaning of this silence?...

[...]
 I re-read your letters the other day, & I will not believe that the man who wrote them did not feel them, & did not know enough of the woman to whom they were written to trust to her love & courage, rather than leave her to this aching uncertainty.
 What has brought about such a change? Oh, no matter what it is—only tell me!
 I could take my life up again courageously if I only understood; for whatever those months were to you, to me they were a great gift, a wonderful enrichment; & still I rejoice

& give thanks for them! You woke me from a long lethargy, a dull acquiescence in conventional restrictions, a needless self-effacement. If I was awkward & inarticulate it was because, literally, all one side of me was asleep.

I remember, that night we went to the 'Figlia di Iorio,' that in the scene in the cave, where the Figlia sends him back to his mother (I forget all their names), & as he goes he turns & kisses her, & then she can't let him go—I remember you turned to me & said laughing: 'That's something you don't know anything about.'

Well! I did know, soon afterward; & if I still remained inexpressive, unwilling, 'always drawing away,' as you said, it was because I discovered in myself such possibilities of feeling on that side that I feared, if I let you love me too much, I might lose courage when the time came to go away!—Surely you saw this, & understood how I dreaded to be to you, even for an instant, the 'donna non più giovane' who clings & encumbers—how, situated as I was, I thought I could best show my love by refraining—& abstaining? You saw it was all because I loved you?

And when you spoke of your uncertain future, your longing to break away & do the work you really like, didn't you see how my heart broke with the thought that, if I had been younger & prettier, everything might have been different—that we might have had together, at least for a short time, a life of exquisite collaborations—a life in which your gifts would have had full scope, & you would have been able to do the distinguished & beautiful things that you ought to do?—Now, I hope, your future has after all arranged itself happily, just as you despaired—but remember that those were my thoughts when you were calling me 'conventional'...

[...]

Yes, dear, I loved you then, & I love you now, as you then wished me to; only I have learned that one must put all the happiness one can into each moment, & I will never again love you 'sadly,' since that displeases you.

You see I am once more assuming that you do care what I feel, in spite of this mystery! How can it be that the sympathy between two people like ourselves, so many-sided, so steeped in imagination, should end from one day to another like a mere 'passade'—end by my passing, within a few weeks, utterly out of your memory? By all that I know you are, by all I am myself conscious of being, I declare that I am unable to believe it!

You told me once I should write better for this experience of loving. I felt it to be so, & I came home so fired by the desire that my work should please you! But this incomprehensible silence, the sense of your utter indifference to everything that concerns me, has stunned me. It has come so suddenly...

This is the last time I shall write you, dear, unless the strange spell is broken. And my last word is one of tenderness for the friend I love—for the lover I worshipped.

Goodbye, dear.

Oh, I don't want my letters back, dearest! I said that in my other letter only to make it easier for you if you were seeking a transition—

Do you suppose I care what becomes of them if you don't care?

Is it really to my dear friend—to Henry's friend—to 'dearest Morton'—that I have written this?

Old love letters are best remembered

Sullivan Ballou to Sarah Ballou

One week before he and thousands of Americans were to die fighting in the First Battle of Bull Run, Major Sullivan Ballou wrote this heart-wrenching letter to his wife, Sarah.

(Washington DC, 14 July 1861)

My very dear Sarah:

The indications are very strong that we shall move in a few days—perhaps tomorrow. Lest I should not be able to write you again, I feel impelled to write lines that may fall under your eye when I shall be no more.

Our movement may be one of a few days duration and full of pleasure—and it may be one of severe conflict and death to me. Not my will, but thine O God, be done. If it is necessary that I should fall on the battlefield for my country, I am ready. I have no misgivings about, or lack of confidence in, the cause in which I am engaged, and my courage does not halt or falter. I know how strongly American Civilization now leans upon the triumph of the Government, and how great a debt we owe to those who went before us through the blood and suffering of the Revolution. And I am willing—perfectly willing—to lay down all my joys in this life, to help maintain this Government, and to pay that debt.

But, my dear wife, when I know that with my own joys I lay down nearly all of yours, and replace them in this life with cares and sorrows—when, after having eaten for long years the bitter fruit of orphanage myself, I must offer it as their only sustenance to my dear little children—is it weak or dishonorable, while the banner of my purpose floats calmly and proudly in the breeze, that my unbounded love for you, my darling wife and children, should struggle in fierce, though useless, contest with my love of country?

I cannot describe to you my feelings on this calm summer night, when two thousand men are sleeping around me, many of them enjoying the last, perhaps, before that of death—and I, suspicious that Death is creeping behind me with his fatal dart, am communing with God, my country, and thee.

I have sought most closely and diligently, and often in my breast, for a wrong motive in thus hazarding the happiness of those I loved and I could not find one. A pure love of my country and of the principles have often advocated before the people and 'the name of honor that I love more than I fear death' have called upon me, and I have obeyed.

Sarah, my love for you is deathless, it seems to bind me to you with mighty cables that nothing but Omnipotence could break; and yet my love of Country comes over me like a strong wind and bears me irresistibly on with all these chains to the battlefield.

The memories of the blissful moments I have spent with you come creeping over me, and I feel most gratified to God and to you that I have enjoyed them so long. And hard it is for me to give them up and burn to ashes the hopes of future years, when God willing, we might still have lived and loved together and seen our sons grow up to honorable manhood around us. I have, I know, but few and small claims upon Divine Providence, but something whispers to me—perhaps it is the wafted prayer of my little Edgar—that I shall return to my loved ones unharmed. If I do not, my dear Sarah, never forget how much I love you, and when my last breath escapes me on the battlefield, it will whisper your name.

Forgive my many faults, and the many pains I have caused you. How thoughtless and foolish I have oftentimes been! How gladly would I wash out with my tears every little spot upon your happiness, and struggle with all the misfortune of this world, to shield you and my children from harm. But I cannot. I must watch you from the spirit land and hover near you, while you buffet the storms with your precious little freight, and wait with sad patience till we meet to part no more.

But, O Sarah! If the dead can come back to this earth and flit unseen around those they loved, I shall always be near you; in the garish day and in the darkest night—amidst your happiest scenes and gloomiest hours—always, always; and if there be a soft breeze upon your cheek, it shall be my breath; or the cool air fans your throbbing temple, it shall be my spirit passing by.

Sarah, do not mourn me dead; think I am gone and wait for thee, for we shall meet again.

As for my little boys, they will grow as I have done, and never know a father's love and care. Little Willie is too young to remember me long, and my blue-eyed Edgar will keep my frolics with him among the dimmest memories of his childhood. Sarah, I have unlimited confidence in your maternal care and your development of their characters. Tell

my two mothers his and hers I call God's blessing upon them. O Sarah, I wait for you there! Come to me, and lead thither my children.
    Sullivan

Old love letters are best remembered

61

Warren G. Harding to Carrie Fulton Phillips

There is a collection of 1,000 pages of love letters between the twenty-ninth US President Warren G. Harding and his mistress Carrie Fulton Phillips. Harding was the Lieutenant Governor of Ohio when he wrote the letter below to his mistress.

(15 September 1913)

[...]
    Wouldn't you like to get sopping wet out on Superior—not the lake—for the joy of fevered fondling and melting kisses? Wouldn't you like to make the suspected occupant of the next room jealous of the joys he could not know, as we did in morning communion at Richmond?
[...]

Old love letters are best remembered

62

Pietro Bembo to Lucrezia Borgia

Pietro Bembo (1470–1547) was one of the most respected poets and scholars of his day, and eventually became a cardinal of the Roman Catholic Church. Born in an aristocratic Venetian family, he had a successful career in politics, the church and the arts. He wrote this letter to Lucrezia Borgia, the daughter of the Spanish cardinal, Rodrigo Borgia, later known as Pope Alexander VI, with whom he was having a passionate love affair.

(Venice, 18 October 1503)

Eight days have passed since I parted from f.f., and already it is as though I had been eight years away from her, although I can avow that not one hour has passed without her memory which has become such a close companion to my thoughts that now more than ever is it the food and sustenance of my soul; and if it should endure like this a few days more, as seems it must, I truly believe it will in every way have assumed the office of my soul, and I shall then live and thrive on the memory of her as do other men upon their souls, and I shall have no life but in this single thought.

Let the God who so decrees do as he will, so long as in exchange I may have as much a part of her as shall suffice to prove the gospel of our affinity is founded on true prophecy. Often I find myself recalling, and with what ease, certain words spoken to me, some on the balcony with the moon as witness, others at that window I shall always look upon so gladly, with all the many endearing and gracious acts I have seen my gentle lady perform—for all are dancing about my heart with a tenderness so wondrous that they inflame me with a strong desire to beg her to test the quality of my love.

For I shall never rest content until I am certain she knows what she is able to enact in me and how great and strong is the fire that her great worth has kindled in my breast. The flame of true love is a mighty force, and most of all when two equally matched wills in two exalted minds contend to see which loves the most, each striving to give yet more vital proof...

It would be the greatest delight for me to see just two lines in f.f.'s hand, yet I dare not ask so much. May your Ladyship beseech her to perform whatever you feel is best for me. With my heart I kiss your Ladyship's hand, since I cannot with my lips.

Old love letters are best remembered

63

Elizabeth Barrett Browning to Robert Browning

Elizabeth Moulton-Barrett (1806–61) was born near Durham, England, and was the eldest among her 12 siblings. She grew up in the countryside, until the Barretts moved to 50 Wimpole Street, London in 1838. She had established herself as a poet by 1845, when Robert Browning began to correspond with her. Her most famous poetry collection, Sonnets from the Portuguese, *was written four years after their elopement and marriage.*

The couple settled in Florence and had a son named Robert Wiedemann Barrett (nicknamed Pen) in 1849, when Elizabeth was 43. Her love story in verse, Aurora Leigh *(1857), was a hugely popular success. Elizabeth's health had always been delicate and gradually became worse. She died on 29 June 1861, and is buried in Florence.*

Robert Browning (1812–89) was a renowned Victorian poet. Born in London, he was the son of a clerk in the Bank of England. His father was in charge of his education, and paid for the printing of his first poems. His early work was obscure; Men and Women *(1855), his first collection of dramatic lyrics, sold very few copies. Disappointed, Browning decided to stop writing to care for his beloved wife. After her death, he picked up writing once again.* Dramatis Personae *(1864) was a success, and it was followed by what is considered his greatest work,*

The Ring and the Book *(1868–69)*. *The latter established him as a literary giant, even though his work was never as popular as Elizabeth's. He died in Venice in 1889 and is buried in Poets' Corner at Westminster Abbey.*

(10 January 1846)

[…]
　…Do you know, when you have told me to think of you, I have been feeling ashamed of thinking of you so much, of thinking of only you—which is too much, perhaps. Shall I tell you? It seems to me, to myself, that no man was ever before to any woman what you are to me—the fulness must be in proportion, you know, to the vacancy…and only I know what was behind—the long wilderness without the blossoming rose…and the capacity for happiness, like a black gaping hole, before this silver flooding. Is it wonderful that I should stand as in a dream, and disbelieve—not you—but my own fate?

　Was ever any one taken suddenly from a lampless dungeon and placed upon the pinnacle of a mountain, without the head turning round and the heart turning faint, as mine do? And you love me more, you say?—Shall I thank you or God? Both,—indeed—and there is no possible return from me to either of you! I thank you as the unworthy may…and as we all thank God. How shall I ever prove what my heart is to you? How will you ever see it as I feel it? I ask myself in vain. Have so much faith in me, my only beloved, as to use me simply for your own advantage and happiness, and to your own ends without a thought of any others—that is all I could ask you without any disquiet as to the granting of it—May God bless you!— Your BA.

Old love letters are best remembered

64

Prince Albert to Queen Victoria

Prince Albert, the consort of Queen Victoria, wrote the sweetest words to his future wife in October of 1839 upon his engagement to Queen Victoria. He once said, 'How is it that I have deserved so much love, so much affection? I cannot get used to the reality of all that I see and hear, and have to believe that heaven has sent me an angel whose brightness shall illumine my life.'

(15 November 1839)

Dearest deeply loved Victoria,

[…]
    I need not tell you that since we left, all my thoughts have been with you at Windsor, and that your image fills my whole soul. Even in my dreams I never imagined that I should find so much love on earth. How that moment shines for me still when I was close to you, with your hand in mine. Those days flew by so quickly, but our separation will fly equally so.

Ernest wishes me to say a thousand nice things to you.
With promises of unchanging love and devotion,
Your ever true

Albert.

Old love letters are best remembered

65

Charlotte Brontë to Professor Constantin Héger

Charlotte Brontë was a famous British poet and novelist. A well-known quote from her novel Jane Eyre *goes: 'I have for the first time found what I can truly love—I found you.'*

(8 January 1845)

[...]
   Monsieur, the poor have not need of much to sustain them—they ask only for the crumbs that fall from the rich man's table. But if they are refused the crumbs they die of hunger. Nor do I, either, need much affection from those I love. I should not know what to do with a friendship entire and complete—I am not used to it. But you showed me of yore a little interest, when I was your pupil in Brussels, and I hold on to the maintenance of that little interest—I hold on to it as I would hold on to life.
   [...]

Old love letters are best remembered

66

Catherine of Aragon to Henry VIII

Catherine of Aragon (1485–1536) was the Queen of England, the first of Henry VIII's six wives and the mother of Queen Mary I. King Henry VIII annulled their marriage in 1533, initiating the English Reformation to marry his paramour, Anne Boleyn, instead. Nevertheless, this letter, written in 1535, shows how devoted Catherine remained to him until her last days.

(1535)

My Lord and Dear Husband,

I commend me unto you. The hour of my death draweth fast on, and my case being such, the tender love I owe you forceth me, with a few words, to put you in remembrance of the health and safeguard of your soul, which you ought to prefer before all worldly matters, and before the care and tendering of your own body, for the which you have cast me into many miseries and yourself into many cares.

For my part I do pardon you all, yea, I do wish and devoutly pray God that He will also pardon you.

For the rest I commend unto you Mary, our daughter, beseeching you to be a good father unto her, as I heretofore desired. I entreat you also, on behalf of my maids, to give them marriage-portions, which is not much, they being but three. For all my other servants, I solicit a year's pay more than their due, lest they should be unprovided for.

Lastly, do I vow, that mine eyes desire you above all things.

∽

Old love letters are best remembered

67

Henry IV of France to Gabrielle d'Estrées

Henry IV of France (1553–1610) was the King of Navarre from 1572 and the first Bourbon king of France from 1589. A skilled negotiator and a brave soldier, he worked hard to unite a country torn by religious divides.

This is a letter he wrote to his mistress, Gabrielle d'Estrées, from the battlefield of Dreux.

(16 June 1593)

I have waited patiently for one whole day without news of you; I have been counting the time and that's what it must be. But a second day—I can see no reason for it, unless my servants have grown lazy or been captured by the enemy, for I dare not put the blame on you, my beautiful angel: I am too confident of your affection—which is certainly due to me, for my love was never greater, nor my desire more urgent; that is why I repeat this refrain in all my letters: come, come, come, my dear love.

Honour with your presence the man who, if only he were free, would go a thousand miles to throw himself at your feet and never move from there. As for what is happening here, we have drained the water from the moat, but our cannons are not going to be in place until Friday when, God willing, I will dine in town.

The day after you reach Mantes, my sister will arrive at Anet, where I will have the pleasure of seeing you every day. I am sending you a bouquet of orange blossom that I have just received. I kiss the hands of the Vicomtess [Gabrielle's sister, Françoise] if she is there, and of my good friend [his sister, Catherine of Bourbon], and as for you, my dear love, I kiss your feet a million times.

⁓

Old love letters are best remembered

68

Ernest Hemingway to Marlene Dietrich

Ernest Hemingway was a famous American short story writer, novelist and journalist.

'I didn't want to kiss you goodbye—that was the trouble—I wanted to kiss you goodnight. And there's a lot of difference.'

'Live the full life of the mind, exhilarated by new ideas, intoxicated by the romance of the unusual.'

(28 August 1955)

Dearest Kraut:

Thanks very much for the good long letter with the gen on what you found wrong. I don't know anything about the theater but I don't think it would occur to me, even, to have you introduced even to me with strains of La Vie En Rose. Poor peoples.

If I were staging it would probably have something novel like having you shot onto the stage, drunk, from a self-propelled minnenwerfer which would advance in from the street rolling over the customers. We would be playing 'Land of Hope and Glory.' As you landed on the stage drunk and naked I would advance from the rear, or from your rear wearing evening clothes and would hurriedly strip off my evening clothes to cover you revealing the physique of Burt Lancaster Strongfort and announce that we were sorry that we did not know the lady was loaded. All this time the Thirty ton S/P/ Mortar would be bulldozing the customers as we break into the Abortion Scene from 'Lakme'. This is a scene which is really Spine Tingling and I have just the spine for it. I play it with a Giant Rubber Whale called Captain Ahab and all the time we are working on you with pulmotors and raversed (sic) cleaners which blow my evening clothes off you. You are foaming at the mouth of course to show that we are really acting and we bottle the foam and sell it to any surviving customers. You are referred to in the contract as The Artist and I am just Captain Ahab. Fortunately I am crazed and I keep shouting 'Fire One. Fire Two. Fire Three.' And don't think we do not fire them. It is then that the Germ of the Mutiny is born in your disheveled brain.

But why should a great Artist-Captain like me invent so many for so few for only air-mail love on Sunday morning when I should be in church. Only for fun, I guess. Gentlemen, crank up your hearses.

Marlene, darling, I write stories but I have no grace for fucking them up for other mediums. It was hard enough for me to learn to write to be read by the human eye. I do not know how, nor do I care to know how to write to be read by parrots, monkeys, apes, baboons, nor actors.

I love you very much and I never wanted to get mixed in any business with you as I wrote you when this thing first was brought up. Neither of us has enough whore blood for that. Not but what I number many splendid whores amongst my best friends and certainly never, I hope, could be accused of anti-whoreism. Not only that but I was circumcised as a very early age.

Hope you have it good in California and Las Vegas. What I hear from the boys is that many people in La Vegas (sic) or three or four anyway of the mains are over-extended. This is very straight gen but everybody knows it if I know it although I have not told anyone what I've heard and don't tell you. But watch all money ends. Some people would as soon have the publicity of making you look bad as of your expected and legitimate success. But that is the way everything is everywhere and no criticism of Nevada or anyone there. Cut this paragraph out of this letter and burn it if you want to keep the rest of the letter in case you thought any of it funny. I rely on you as a Kraut officer and gentlemen do this.

New Paragraph. I love you very much and wish you luck. Wish me some too. Book is on page 592. This week Thursday we start photography on fishing. Am in charge of fishing etc. and it is going to be difficult enough. With a bad back a little worse. The Artist is not here naturally. I only wrote the book but must do the work as well and have no stand-in. Up at 0450 knock off at 1930. This goes on for 15 days.

I think you could say you and I have earned whatever dough the people let us keep.

So what. So Merdre. I love you as always.

Papa

Old love letters are best remembered

69

Vincent van Gogh to Theo van Gogh (About His Cousin 'Kee')

The famous Dutch artist Vincent van Gogh wrote this letter to his brother, Theo, describing his passion for his cousin, Cornelia 'Kee' Adriana Vos-Stricker. She rejected Vincent's proposal of marriage, and never changed her position of 'no, never never'.

(7 November 1881)

[...]
    Life has become very dear to me, and I am very glad that I love. My life and my love are one. 'But you are faced with a "no, never never"' is your reply. My answer to that is, 'Old boy, for the present I look upon that "no, never never" as a block of ice which I press to my heart to thaw.'
    [...]

Old love letters are best remembered

70

Heinrich von Kleist to Adolfine Henriette Vogel

Heinrich von Kleist was a German dramatist and poet. He wrote this letter to his sweetheart, Adolfine Henriette Vogel, who was suffering from an incurable disease.

(1810)

[…]
   My golden child, my pearl, my precious stone, my crown, my queen and empress. You dear darling of my heart, my highest and most precious, my all and everything, my wife, the baptism of my children, my tragic play, my posthumous reputation. Ach! You are my second better self, my virtues, my merits, my hope, the forgiveness of my sins, my future sanctity, O little daughter of heaven, my child of God, my intercessor, my guardian angel, my cherubim and seraph, how I love you!...

Old love letters are best remembered

71

Oliver Cromwell to Elizabeth Cromwell

Oliver Cromwell was an English politician and military officer who is widely regarded as one of the most important statesmen in English history.

'Let your heart crumble into an infinite amount of tiny, precious seeds. Then plant love everywhere you go.'

(Dunbar, 4 September 1650)

MY DEAREST,

I have not leisure to write much. But I could chide thee that in many of thy letters thou writest to me, that I should not be unmindful of thee and thy little ones. Truly, if I love you not too well, I think I err not on the other hand much. Thou art dearer to me than any creature; let that suffice.

The Lord hath showed us an exceeding mercy:—who can tell how great it is! My weak faith hath been upheld. I have been in my inward man marvellously supported;—though I assure thee, I grow an old man, and feel infirmities of age marvellously stealing upon me. Would my corruptions did as fast decrease! Pray on my behalf in the latter respect. The particulars of our late success Harry Vane or Gilbert Pickering will impart to thee. My love to all dear friends.

    I rest thine,

OLIVER CROMWELL.

(Edinburgh, 3 May 1651)

MY DEAREST,

I could not satisfy myself to omit this post, although I have not much to write; yet indeed I love to write to my Dear, who is very much in my heart. It joys me to hear thy soul prospereth: the Lord increase His favours to thee more and more. The great good thy soul can wish is, That the Lord lift upon thee the light of His countenance, which is better than life. The Lord bless all thy good counsel and example to all those about thee, and hear all thy prayers, and accept thee always.

    I am glad to hear thy Son and Daughter are with thee. I hope thou wilt have some good opportunity of good advice to him. Present my duty to my Mother, my love to all the Family.

    Still pray for

Thine,
OLIVER CROMWELL.

Old love letters are best remembered

72

Jane Baillie Welsh to Thomas Carlyle

This letter was the last one that Jane Baillie Welsh wrote to famous Scottish essayist and historian, Thomas Carlyle, before they got married.

(3 October 1826)

[…] it is so easy a thing for you to lift me to Seventh Heaven! My soul was darker than midnight, when your pen said 'let there be light.' and there was light as at the bidding of the Word. […] When I read in your looks and words that you love me, I feel it in the deepest part of my soul; and then I care not one straw for the whole Universe beside […]

Old love letters are best remembered

73

Jack London to Anna Strunsky

Jack London, American author of The Call of the Wild *and* White Fang, *was one of the first writers ever to achieve celebrity status. A quote from one of his stories goes: 'Love, genuine passionate love, was his for the first time.'*

(Oakland, 3 April 1901)

[...]
Did I say that the human might be filed in categories? Well, and if I did, let me qualify—not all humans. You elude me. I cannot place you, cannot grasp you. I may boast that of nine out of ten, under given circumstances, I can forecast their action; that of nine out of ten, by their word or action, I may feel the pulse of their hearts. But of the tenth I despair. It is beyond me. You are that tenth.
[...]

Old love letters are best remembered

74

Woodrow Wilson to Edith Galt Wilson

Woodrow Wilson was the twenty-eighth president of the United States, from 1913 to 1921. Edith Bolling Galt, later Edith Galt Wilson, was his second wife, and first lady of the United States from 1915 until the end of her husband's term.

(The White House, 19 September 1915)

My noble, incomparable Edith,

I do not know how to express or analyze the conflicting emotions that have surged like a storm through my heart all night long. I only know that first and foremost in all my thoughts has been the glorious confirmation you gave me last night—without effort, unconsciously, as of course—of all I have ever thought of your mind and heart.

You have the greatest soul, the noblest nature, the sweetest, most loving heart I have ever known, and my love, my reverence, my admiration for you, you have increased in one evening as I should have thought only a lifetime of intimate, loving association could have increased them.

You are more wonderful and lovely in my eyes than you ever were before; and my pride and joy and gratitude that you should love me with such a perfect love are beyond all expression, except in some great poem which I cannot write.

Your own,
Woodrow

Old love letters are best remembered

Dorothy Osborne to Sir William Temple

Dorothy Osborne, daughter of Sir Peter Osborne, was born in 1627 in Bedfordshire, England. She is famous for the letters that she wrote to her future husband, William Temple, whom she married in 1655 despite their families opposing the match. The couple had nine children, of whom two survived past infancy.

Osborne's letters reveal her wit and the depth of her reading, filled with curious and insightful references to literature. Her correspondence with Temple seems to have been her safe haven, where she could connect deeper with him away from prying eyes, surrounded only by his words. Indeed, as she states, 'You are enough in my heart to know all my thoughts…'

SIR,

I have been reckoning up how many faults you lay to my charge in your last letter, and I find I am severe, unjust, unmerciful, and unkind. Oh me, how should one do to mend all these! 'Tis work for an age, and 'tis to be feared I shall be so old before I am good, that 'twill not be considerable to anybody but myself whether I am so or not. I say nothing of the pretty humour you fancied me in, in your dream, because 'twas but a dream. Sure, if it had been anything else, I should have remembered that my Lord L. loves to have his chamber and his bed to himself. But seriously, now, I wonder at your patience. How could you hear me talk so senselessly, though 'twere but in your sleep, and not to be ready to beat me? What nice mistaken points of honour I pretend to, and yet could allow him a room in the same bed with me! Well, dreams are pleasant things to people whose humours are so; but to have the spleen, and to dream upon't, is a punishment I would not wish my greatest enemy. I seldom dream, or never remember them, unless they have been so sad as to put me into such disorder as I can hardly recover when I am awake, and some of those I am confident I shall never forget.

You ask me how I pass my time here. I can give you a perfect account not only of what I do for the present, but of what I am likely to do this seven years if I stay here so long. I rise in the morning reasonably early, and before I am ready I go round the house till I am weary of that, and then into the garden till it grows too hot for me. About ten o'clock I think of making me ready, and when that's done I go into my father's chamber, from thence to dinner, where my cousin Molle and I sit in great state in a room and at a table that would hold a great many more. After dinner we sit and talk till Mr. B. comes in question, and then I am gone. The heat of the day is spent in reading or working, and about six or seven o'clock I walk out into a common that lies hard by the house, where a great many young wenches keep sheep and cows, and sit in the shade singing of ballads. I go to them and compare their voices and beauties to some ancient shepherdesses that I have read of, and find a vast difference there; but, trust me I think these are as innocent as those could be. I talk to them, and find they want nothing to make them the happiest people in the world but the knowledge that they are so. Most commonly, when we are in the midst of our discourse, one looks about her, and spies her cows going into the corn, and then away they all run as if they had wings at their heels. I, that am not so nimble, stay behind; and when I see them driving home their cattle, I think 'tis time for me to retire too. When I have supped, I go into the garden, and so to the side of a small river that runs by it, where I sit down and wish you with me (you had best say this is not kind neither). In earnest, 'tis a pleasant place, and would be much more so to me if I had your company. I sit there sometimes till I am lost with thinking; and were it not for some cruel thoughts of the crossness of our fortunes that will not let me sleep there, I should forget that there were such a thing to be done as going to bed.

Since I writ this my company is increased by two, my brother Harry and a fair niece, the eldest of my brother Peyton's daughters. She is so much a woman that I am almost ashamed to say I am her aunt; and so pretty, that if I had any design to gain a servant, I should not like her company; but I have none, and therefore shall endeavour to keep her here as long as I can persuade her father to spare her, for she will easily consent to it, having so much of my humour (though it be the worst thing in her) as to like a melancholy place and little company. My brother John is not come down again, nor am I certain when he will be here. He went from London into Gloucestershire to my sister who was very ill, and his youngest girl, of which he was very fond, is since dead. But I believe by that time his wife has a little recovered her sickness and the loss of her child, he will be coming this way. My father is reasonably well, but keeps his chamber still, and will hardly, I am afraid, ever be so perfectly recovered as to come abroad again.

I am sorry for poor Walker, but you need not doubt of what he has of yours in his hands, for it seems he does not use to do his work himself. I speak seriously, he keeps a Frenchman that sets all his seals and rings. If what you say of my Lady Leppington be of your own knowledge, I shall believe you, but otherwise I can assure you I have heard from people that pretend to know her very well, that her kindness to Compton was very moderate, and that she never liked him so well as when he died and gave her his estate. But they might be deceived, and 'tis not so strange as that you should imagine a coldness and an indifference in my letters where I so little meant it; but I am not displeased you should desire my kindness enough to apprehend the loss of it when it is safest. Only I would not have you apprehend it so far as to believe it possible—that were an injury to all the assurances I have given you, and if you love me you cannot think me unworthy. I should think myself so, if I found you grew indifferent to me, that I have had so long and so particular a friendship for; but, sure, this is more than I need to say. You are enough in my heart to know all my thoughts, and if so, you know better than I can tell you how much I am

Yours

Old love letters are best remembered

76

Harriet Beecher Stowe to Calvin Ellis Stowe

Harriet Beecher Stowe (1811–96) found immediate success and controversy with her first novel, Uncle Tom's Cabin, *written in 1852. After surviving that firestorm, she went on to publish eight more novels and dozens of short stories. She enjoyed a happy, albeit busy, home life with her husband, Calvin, and their six children. In this letter, written eleven years after their wedding, Stowe reflects on the joy and tribulations she shared with her husband.*

'...the heart has no tears to give,—it drops only blood, bleeding itself away in silence.'

'Love needs new leaves every summer of life, as much as your elm tree, and new branches to go broader and wider, and new flowers to cover the ground.'

(1 January 1847)

My Dearest Husband

...I was at that date of marriage a very different being from what I am now and stood in relation to my Heavenly Father in a very different attitude. My whole desire was to live in love, absorbing passionate devotion to one person. Our separation was my first trial—but then came a note of comfort in the hope of being a mother. No creature ever so longed to see the face of a little one or had such a heart full of love to bestow. Here came in trial again sickness, pain, perplexity, constant discouragement—wearing wasting days and nights—a cross, deceitful, unprincipled nurse—husband gone... When you came back you came only to increasing perplexities.

Ah, how little comfort I had in being a mother—how was all that I proposed met and crossed and my way ever hedged up!

...In short, God would teach me that I should make no family be my chief good and portion and bitter as the lesson has been I thank Him for it from my very soul. One might naturally infer that from the union of two both morbidly sensitive and acute, yet in many respects exact opposites—one hasty and impulsive—the other sensitive and brooding—one the very personification of exactness and routine and the other to whom everything of the kind was an irksome effort—from all this what should one infer but some painful friction.

But all this would not after all have done so very much had not Providence as if intent to try us throws upon the heaviest external pressure...but still where you have failed your faults have been to me those of one beloved—of the man who after all would be the choice of my heart still were I to choose—for were I now free I should again love just as I did and again feel that I could give up all to and for you— and if I do not love never can love again with the blind and unwise love with which I married I love quite as truly tho far more wisely...

In reflecting upon our future union—our marriage—the past obstacles to our happiness—it seems to me that they are of two or three kinds. 1st those from physical causes both in you and in me—such on your part as hypochondriac morbid instability for which the only remedy is physical care and attention to the laws of health—and on my part an excess of sensitiveness and of confusion and want of control of mind and memory. This always increases on my part in proportion as a I am blamed and found fault with and I hope will decrease with returning health. I hope that we shall both be impressed with a most solemn sense of the importance of a wise and constant attention to the laws of health.

Then in the second place the want of any definite plan of mutual watchfulness, with regard to each other's improvement, of a definite time and place for doing it with a firm determination to improve and be improved by each other—to confess our faults one to another and pray one for another that we may be healed...

Yours with much love
H.

Old love letters are best remembered

77

Herman Melville to Nathaniel Hawthorne

Herman Melville was a famous American short story writer, novelist and poet of the Renaissance Era. He once said: 'We cannot live only for ourselves.'

(November 1851)

[...] your heart beat in my ribs and mine in yours, and both in God's. [...] It is a strange feeling—no hopefulness is in it, no despair. Content—that is it; and irresponsibility; but without licentious inclination. I speak now of my profoundest sense of being, not of an incidental feeling.

Whence come you, Hawthorne? By what right do you drink from my flagon of life? And when I put it to my lips—lo, they are yours and not mine. I feel that the Godhead is broken up like the bread at the Supper, and that we are the pieces.

[...]

My dear Hawthorne, the atmospheric skepticisms steal into me now, and make me doubtful of my sanity in writing you thus. But, believe me, I am not mad, most noble Festus! But truth is ever incoherent, and when the big hearts strike together, the concussion is a little stunning.

[...]

P.S. I can't stop yet. If the world was entirely made up of [magicians], I'll tell you what I should do. I should have a paper-mill established at one end of the house, and so have an endless riband of foolscap rolling in upon my desk; and upon that endless riband I should write a thousand—a million—billion thoughts, all under the form of a letter to you. The divine magnet is in you, and my magnet responds. Which is the biggest? A foolish question—they are One.

[...]

Old love letters are best remembered

78

Mary Wollstonecraft to Gilbert Imlay

Mary Wollstonecraft and Gilbert Imlay met in 1793, soon after she had published her famous feminist work, A Vindication of the Rights of Woman. *In the spirit of her progressive views on female sexuality and equality, she was the one who acted on her attraction and initiated their romance.*

The two did not want to conform to society's standards of a relationship and believed in free love. As a result, they had a daughter, Fanny, out of wedlock.

However, their relationship was unable to last, with Imlay not wanting marriage and Wollstonecraft later discovering that he had a mistress. She became deeply depressed and had to take a break from her activism. Nevertheless, the first line of a letter from their passionate days is simply the dictate of the Heart: 'I obey an emotion of my heart...'.

Given below are two letters: one that Wollstonecraft wrote to Imlay in the initial stages of their romance, and one that confirmed their break-up.

(August 1793)

To Gilbert Imlay,

I obey an emotion of my heart, which made me think of wishing thee, my love, goodnight! before I go to rest, with more tenderness that I can to-morrow, when writing a hasty line or two under Colonel ——'s eyes. You can imagine with what pleasure I antiicipate the day when we are to begin almost to live together; and you would smile to hear how many plans of employment I have in my head, now that I am confident my heart has found peace in your bosom. Cherish me with that dignified tenderness, which I have only found in you; and your own dear girl will try to keep under a quickness of feeling, that has sometimes given you pain-Yes, I will be good, that I may deserve to be happy; and whilst you to love me, I cannot again fall into the miserable state which rendered life a burden almost too heavy too burden.

But good night! God bless you! Sterne says, that is equal to a kiss—yet I would rather give you the kiss into the bargain, glowing with gratitude to Heaven and affection to you. I like the word affection, because it signifies something habitual; and we are soon to meet, to try whether we have mind enough to keep our hearts warm.

Mary

(10 October 1795)

To Gilbert Imlay,

I write you now on my knees; imploring you to send my child and the maid to Paris, to be consigned to the care of Madam ——. Should they be removed —— can give their direction.

Let the maid have my clothes, without distinction. Pray pay the cook her wages, and do not mention the confession which

I forced from her—a little sooner or later is of no consequence. Nothing but my extreme stupidity could have rendered me blind so long. Yet, whilst you assured me that you had no attachment, I thought we might still have lived together.

I shall make no comments on your conduct; or any appeal to the world. Let my wrongs sleep with me! Soon, very soon, shall I be at peace. When you receive this, my burning head will be cold. I would encounter a thousand deaths, rather than a night like the last. Your treatment has thrown my mind into a state of chaos; yet I am serene.

I go find comfort, and my only fear is, that my poor body will be insulted by an endeavour to recall my hated existence. But I shall plunge into the Thames where there is the least chance of my being snatched from the death I seek.

God bless you! May I never know by experience what you have made me endure. Should your sensibility ever awake, remorse will find its way to your heart; and, in the midst of business and sensual pleasures, I shall appear before you, the victim of your deviation from rectitude.

Mary

Old love letters are best remembered

Captain Frederick Wentworth to Anne Elliot

Captain Frederick Wentworth is a fictional character from the novel Persuasion *by Jane Austen. This is how Austen sets the scene: 'Wentworth drew out a letter from under the scattered paper, placed it before Anne with eyes of glowing entreaty, fixed on her for a time.'*

I can listen no longer in silence. I must speak to you by such means as are within my reach. You pierce my soul. I am half agony, half hope. Tell me not that I am too late, that such precious feelings are gone for ever. I offer myself to you again with a heart even more your own than when you almost broke it, eight years and a half ago. Dare not say that man forgets sooner than woman, that his love has an earlier death. I have loved none but you. Unjust I may have been, weak and resentful I have been, but never inconstant. You alone have brought me to Bath. For you alone, I think and plan. Have you not seen this? Can you fail to have understood my wishes? I had not waited even these ten days, could I have read your feelings, as I think you must have penetrated mine. I can hardly write. I am every instant hearing something which overpowers me. You sink your voice, but I can distinguish the tones of that voice when they would be lost on others. Too good, too excellent creature! You do us justice, indeed. You do believe that there is true attachment and constancy among men. Believe it to be most fervent, most undeviating, in F.W.

I must go, uncertain of my fate; but I shall return hither, or follow your party, as soon as possible. A word, a look, will be enough to decide whether I enter your father's house this evening or never.

Old love letters are best remembered

Love Letters in Thomas Hardy's Poetry

Thomas Hardy was one of the most prolific and well-known British novelists and poets of the nineteenth and the twentieth centuries, also known as a war poet. He expressed his emotions not in prose but in poetry. He stated: 'Love is a possible strength in an actual weakness.'

The Love-Letters

(In Memoriam H.R.)

I met him quite by accident
In a bye-path that he'd frequent.
And, as he neared, the sunset glow
Warmed up the smile of pleasantry
Upon his too thin face, while he
Held a square packet up to me,
Of what, I did not know.

'Well,' said he then; 'they are my old letters.
Perhaps she—rather felt them fetters…
You see, I am in a slow decline,
And she's broken off with me. Quite right

To send them back, and true foresight;
I'd got too fond of her! To-night
I burn them—stuff of mine!'

He laughed in the sun—an ache in his laughter—
And went. I heard of his death soon after.

Old love letters are best remembered

81

Franz Liszt to Marie D'Agoult

Born in 1811, Franz Liszt was a Hungarian composer who became one of the greatest virtuoso pianists of the nineteenth century. His compositions, such as the Piano Sonata in B and the Dante Symphony, *took Paris by storm. While performing in the city, he became acquainted with Countess D'Agoult, a young and beautiful woman who was going through a separation after an unhappy marriage. They fell deeply in love with each other and eventually became a couple, filling each other's hearts with 'heavenly languor'.*

(1834, Thursday morning)

My heart overflows with emotion and joy! I do not know what heavenly languor, what infinite pleasure permeates it and burns me up. It is as if I had never loved!!! Tell me whence these uncanny disturbances spring, these inexpressible foretastes of delight, these divine, tremors of love. Oh! all this can only spring from you, sister, angel, woman, Marie! All this can only be, is surely nothing less than a gentle ray streaming from your fiery soul, or else some secret poignant teardrop which you have long since left in my breast.

My God, my God, never force us apart, take pity on us! But what am I saying? Forgive my weakness, how couldst Thou divide us! Thou wouldst have nothing but pity for us... No no! It is not in vain that our flesh and our souls quicken and become immortal through Thy Word, which cries out deep within us Father, Father...out Thy hand to us, that our broken hearts seek their refuge in Thee...O! we thank, bless and praise Thee, O God, for all that Thou has given us, and all that Thou hast prepared for us....

This is to be—to be!

Marie! Marie!

Oh let me repeat that name a hundred times, a thousand times over; for three days now it has lived within me, oppressed me, set me afire. I am not writing to you, no, I am close beside you. I see you, I hear you. Eternity in your arms... Heaven, Hell, everything, all is within you, redoubled... Oh! Leave me free to rave in my delirium. Drab, tame, constricting reality is no longer enough for me. We must live our lives to the full, loving and suffering to extremes!...

Franz

Old love letters are best remembered

Charles Dickens to Maria Beadnell

Charles Dickens was a British writer and many regarded him as the greatest novelist of the Victorian Era. He created some of the most outstanding fictional characters in the world.

In his novel Great Expectations, *he wrote, 'Love her, love her, love her! If she favours you, love her. If she wounds you, love her. If she tears your heart to pieces—and as it gets older and stronger, it will tear deeper—love her, love her, love her!'*

He also wrote: 'Have a heart that never hardens and a temper that never tires, and a touch that never hurts.'

(1833)

[...]

And now to the object of my present note. I have considered and reconsidered the matter, and I have come to the unqualified determination that I will allow no feeling of pride, no haughty dislike to making a conciliation to prevent my expressing it without reserve. I will advert to nothing that has passed; I will not again seek to excuse any part I have acted or to justify it by any course you have ever pursued; I will revert to nothing that has ever passed between us,—I will only openly and at once say that there is nothing I have more at heart, nothing I more sincerely and earnestly desire, than to be reconciled to you.—It would be useless for me to repeat here what I have so often said before; it would be equally useless to look forward and state my hopes for the future—all that any one can do to raise himself by his own exertions and unceasing assiduity I have done, and will do. I have no guide by which to ascertain your present feelings and I have, God knows, no means of influencing them in my favor. I never have loved and I never can love any human creature breathing but yourself. We have had many differences, and we have lately been entirely separated. Absence, however, has not altered my feelings in the slightest degree, and the Love I now tender you is as pure and as lasting as at any period of our former correspondence. [...]

Old love letters are best remembered

Love Letters in William Butler Yeats' Poetry

William Butler Yeats (W.B. Yeats) was an Irish writer, poet and dramatist and one of the most prominent literary figures of the twentieth century.
　　An excerpt from his poem 'When You Are Old' goes:

How many loved your moments of glad grace,
And loved your beauty with love false or true
But one man loved the pilgrim soul in you,
And loved the sorrows of your changing face.

Love Song
　　My love, we will go, we will go, I and you,
　　And away in the woods we will scatter the dew;
　　And the salmon behold, and the ousel too,
　　My love, we will hear, I and you, we will hear,
　　The calling afar of the doe and the deer.
　　And the bird in the branches will cry for us clear,
　　And the cuckoo unseen in his festival mood;
　　And death, oh my fair one, will never come near
　　In the bosom afar of the fragrant wood.

Old love letters are best remembered

84

Anne Boleyn to Henry VIII

Anne Boleyn lived a short, unhappy life, and her marriage was embittered with jealousy. Even though King Henry VIII had gone to great lengths to marry her, he became unhappy with her because of her coquettish ways; and after she gave birth to two stillborn boys, he became further disenchanted with her. He was soon enamoured with Jane Seymour instead, and was eager to get rid of Boleyn as soon as possible. Her fall from grace was swift—within the month of May 1536 she went from tossing her handkerchief to a lord at May Day festivties, to being beheaded on 19 May, found guilty of adultery, incest and treason.

The letter given below was allegedly written by Anne after she was imprisoned and awaiting trial, and demonstrates her bravery, capability and dignity in mortal danger. Her guilt or innocence may be debatable, but it is clear to see that a brilliant life was cut tragically short by the whims and fancies of an unjust and tyrannical monarch.

(6 May 1536)

SIR,

Your grace's displeasure, and my imprisonment, are things so strange unto me, as what to write, or what to excuse, I am altogether ignorant. Whereas you send unto me (willing me to confess a truth, and so obtain your favour) by such an one whom you know to be mine antient professed enemy; I no sooner received this message by him, than I rightly conceived your meaning, and if, as you say, Confessing a truth indeed may procure my safety, I shall with all willingness and duty perform your command.

But let not your grace ever imagine that your poor wife will ever be brought to acknowledge a fault, where not so much a thought thereof preceded. And to speak a truth, never prince had wife more loyal in all duty, and in all true affection, than you have ever found in Anne Boleyn, with which name and place I could willingly have contented myself, if God and your grace's pleasure had been so pleased. Neither did I at any time so far forget myself in my exaltation, or received queenship, but that I always looked for such an alteration as now I find; for the ground of my preferment being on no surer foundation than your grace's fancy, the least alteration, I knew, was fit and sufficient to draw that fancy to some other subject. You have chosen me from a low estate to be your queen and companion, far beyond my desert or desire. If then, you found me worthy of such honour, good your grace let not any light fancy, or bad counsel of mine enemies, withdraw your princely favour from me; neither let that stain, that unworthy stain of a disloyal heart, towards your good grace, ever cast so foul a blot on your most dutiful wife, and the infant princess, your daughter; try me, good king, but let me have a lawful trial, and let not my sworn enemies sit as my accusers and judges; yea, let me receive an open trial, for my truth shall fear no open shame; then shall you see, either mine innocency cleared, your suspicion and conscience satisfied, the ignominy and slander of the world stopped, or my guilt openly declared. So that, whatsoever God or you may determine of me, your grace may be freed from an open censure; and mine offence being so lawfully proved, your grace is at liberty, both before God and man, not only to execute worthy punishment on me as an unlawful wife, but to follow your affection already settled on that party, for whose sake I am now as I am, whose name I could some good while since have pointed unto; your grace being not ignorant of my suspicion therein.

But, if you have already determined of me, and that only my death, but an infamous slander must bring you the enjoying of your desired happiness; then I desire of God, that he will pardon your great sin therein, and likewise mine enemies, the instruments thereof; and that he will not call you to a strict account for your unprincely and cruel usage of me, at his general judgment-seat, where both you and myself must shortly appear, and in whose judgment, I doubt not (whatsoever the world may think of me), mine innocence shall be openly known, and sufficiently cleared.

My last and only request shall be, that myself may only bear the burden of your grace's displeasure, and that it may not touch the innocent souls of those poor gentlemen, who, as I understand, are likewise in strait imprisonment for my sake. If ever I have found favour in your sight; if ever the name of Anne Boleyn hath been pleasing in your ears, then let me obtain this request, and I will so leave to trouble your grace any further, with mine earnest prayers to the Trinity to have your grace in his good keeping, and to direct you in all your actions. From my doleful prison in the Tower, this sixth of May.

Your most loyal and ever faithful wife,
ANNE BOLEYN

Old love letters are best remembered

85

John Rodgers to Minerva Denison

Captain John Rodgers, born 11 July 1772, was a senior officer in the US Navy. He joined the navy in 1798, soon after it was established, participating in many key military operations during his 40 years of service.

At the age of 30, Rodgers met 17-year-old Minerva Denison at a party, and even though he did not make the best first impression, he soon won over both Denison and her mother with his kindness. The letter below was written while Rodgers had gone to Washington Navy Yard to report for duty, a month after Denison had accepted his marriage proposal.

(Navy Yard, Washington, 2 January 1804)

Ever Charming Girl

I arriv'd here on Sunday the First day of the present year, and now acknowledge with no less pride, than gratitude, that the Fair, chaste, unartful and Generous sentiments you express'd at our last parting can only be portray'd in your own likeness; and be assured that I shall forever set a Value on them <u>such</u> as Time, variety and a change of scenes, will assist me in appreciating with that unbounded respect and admiration which will always elevate you above every sordid View or earthly influence; and my Dear Minerva I do declare before the supreme altar of heaven that I would prefer ten thousand execrating Deaths sooner than knowingly subject myself to conduct which can in any way give you pain, or reason ever to repent your condescension to my wishes; I make those confessions, not only because it affords me pleasure, but to prove that I know how to estimate your Submission to my prayers; but I have still one request to make, <u>which is</u>, that you will have the condescension to consider whether it is necessary that a long twelve months should Elapse before I have the honor and happiness to receive your fair hand; If there is a real necessity for such postponement, I will patiently submit, yet permit me to entreat you to have compassion, as I now, <u>Involuntarily</u>, feel myself placed in the situation of a Fond lover with all the cares and anxieties of a doating husband <u>when</u> separated from a wife that is dearer to him than his own existence—Washington is, at present, very gay; yet I have been very little in the circle of gaiety since I saw you last, as all my leisure moments from my Duty (to my country) are solely engrosed by contemplations of you; every thing I do or hear becomes more and more indifferent when compared with the interest I feel in every thing that concerns you—I am so immersed in thought that I am scarcely able to write or, even, to speak; I therefore beg you to pardon this short scrawl and the next shall be better—

I am my Dear Minerva with all the Tender regards of a fond lover

yours Forever
Jn Rodgers

PS Pray present my best regards to your good Mother and I would request you to do the same for me to Kitty Thomas if it was not inconsistent, for I love Kitty because I believe she loves you

Yours faithfully
R

Old love letters are best remembered

Love Letters in Dante Gabriel Rossetti's Poetry

Dante Gabriel Rossetti was a British painter, poet, translator and illustrator. He was a poet and artist at the same time, and his leitmotif in both his poetry and art was yellow, something that was common among the Pre-Raphaelite poets.

Sonnet XI: The Love-Letter

Warmed by her hand and shadowed by her hair
As close she leaned and poured her heart through thee,
Whereof the articulate throbs accompany
The smooth black stream that makes thy whiteness fair,—
Sweet fluttering sheet, even of her breath aware,—
Oh let thy silent song disclose to me
That soul wherewith her lips and eyes agree
Like married music in Love's answering air.
Fain had I watched her when, at some fond thought,
Her bosom to the writing closelier press'd,
And her breast's secrets peered into her breast;
When, through eyes raised an instant, her soul sought
My soul, and from the sudden confluence caught
The words that made her love the loveliest.

Old love letters are best remembered

Love Letters in Robert Herrick's Poetry

Robert Herrick was an English lyric poet and an Anglican cleric of the seventeenth century, famous for writing Hesperides, *a book of poems.*

A well-known excerpt from one of his poems goes:

Give me a kiss, and to that kiss a score;
Then to that twenty, add a hundred more;
A thousand to that hundred; so kiss on,
To make that thousand up a million.

To Sylvia, to Wed

Let us, though late, at last, my Silvia, wed;
And loving lie in one devoted bed.
Thy watch may stand, my minutes fly post haste;
No sound calls back the year that once is past.
Then, sweetest Silvia, let's no longer stay;
True love, we know, precipitates delay.
Away with doubts, all scruples hence remove!
No man, at one time, can be wise, and love.

Of Love: A Sonnet

How love came in I do not know,
Whether by the eye, or ear, or no;
Or whether with the soul it came
(At first) infused with the same;
Whether in part 'tis here or there,
Or, like the soul, whole everywhere,
This troubles me: but I as well
As any other this can tell:
That when from hence she does depart
The outlet then is from the heart.

His Tears to Thamesis

I send, I send here my supremest kiss
To thee my silver-footed Thamesis.
No more shall I reiterate thy Strand,
Whereon so many stately structures stand;
Nor in the summer's sweeter evenings go
To bathe in thee, as thousand others do;

No more shall I along thy crystal glide
In barge with boughs and rushes beautified,
With soft-smooth virgins (for our chaste disport)
To Richmond, Kingston, and to Hampton Court.
Never again shall I with finny oar
Put from, or draw unto the faithful shore;
And landing here, or safely landing there,
Make way to my beloved Westminster,

Or to the golden Cheapside, where the earth
Of Julia Herrick gave to me my birth.
May all clean nymphs and curious water dames,
With swan-like state, float up and down thy streams;
No drought upon thy wanton waters fall
To make them lean and languishing at all.
No ruffling winds come hither to disease
Thy pure and silver-wristed Naiades.
Keep up your state, ye streams; and as ye spring,
Never make sick your banks by surfeiting.
Grow young with tides, and though I see ye never,
Receive this vow: 'so fare-ye-well forever'

Old love letters are best remembered

Love Letters in Ben Jonson's Poetry

Benjamin 'Ben' Jonson is one of the best-known theorists and writers of English Renaissance literature. He was a man of letters and a prolific dramatist.
Here are some of his famous lines on love:

> 'Come, my Celia, let us prove, while we can, the sports of love.'

> 'Drink to me only with thine eyes,
> And I will pledge with mine;
> Or leave a kiss but in the cup,
> And I will not look for wine.'

> 'Court a mistress, she denies you; let her alone, she will court you.'

Why I Write Not of Love

> Some act of Love's bound to reherse,
> I thought to bind him, in my verse:
> Which when he felt, Away (quoth he)
> Can Poets hope to fetter me?
> It is enough, they once did get

Mars, and my Mother, in their net:
I weare not these my wings in vaine.
With which he fled me: and againe,
Into my rimes could ne're be got
By any art. Then wonder not,
That since, my numbers are so cold,
When Love is fled, and I grow old.

Old love letters are best remembered

89

Katherine Mansfield to John Middleton Murry

Katherine Mansfield was a New Zealand-born writer, essayist and journalist. She is regarded as one of the most influential authors of the modernist movement, with her works published in 25 languages and celebrated worldwide.

Here are some of her famous quotes on love:

'The mind I love must have wild places...'

'Everything in life that we really accept undergoes a change. So suffering must become love. That is the mystery.'

'This is not a letter, but my arms about you for a brief moment.'

'The whole world shall be ours because of our love.'

∫

(Saturday night, 18 May 1917)

My darling,

Do not imagine, because you find these lines in your journal that I have been trespassing. You know I have not—and where else shall I leave a love letter? For I long to write you a love-letter tonight.

You are all about me—I seem to breathe you, hear you, feel you in me and of me.

What am I doing here? You are away. I have seen you in the train, at the station, driving up, sitting in the lamplight, talking, greeting people, washing your hands... And I am here—in your tent—sitting at your table.

There are some wall-flower petals on the table and a dead match, a blue pencil and a *Magdeburgische Zeitung*. I am just as much at home as they.

When dusk came, flowing up the silent garden, lapping against the blind windows, my first and last terror started up. I was making some coffee in the kitchen. It was so violent, so dreadful I put down the coffee pot—and simply ran away—ran out of the studio and up the street with my bag under one arm and a block of writing paper and a pen under the other. I felt that if I could get here and find Mrs. F I should be 'safe'.

I found her and I lighted your gas, wound up your clock, drew your curtains and embraced your black overcoat before I sat down, frightened no longer. Do not be angry with me, Bogey. *Ca a ete plus fort que moi...* That is why I am here.

When you came to tea this afternoon you took a brioche, broke it in half and padded the inside doughy bit with two fingers. You always do that with a bun or roll or a piece of bread. It is your way—your head a little on one side the while.

When you opened your suitcase, I saw your old Feltie and a French book and a comb all higgledy-piggledy. 'Tig, I've only got 3 handkerchiefs.' Why should that memory be so sweet to me?...

Last night, there was a moment before you got into bed. You stood, quite naked, bending forward a little, talking. It was only for an instant. I saw you—I loved you so, loved your body with such tenderness. Ah, my dear!

And I am not thinking of 'passion'. No, of that other thing that makes me feel that every inch of you is so precious to me—your soft shoulders—your creamy warm skin, your ears cold like shells are cold—your long legs and your feet that I love to clasp with my feet—the feeling of your belly—and your thin young back. Just below that bone that sticks out at the back of your neck you have a little mole.

It is partly because we are young that I feel this tenderness. I love your mouth. I could not bear that it should be touched even by a cold wind if I were the Lord.

We two, you know, have everything before us, and we shall do very great things. I have perfect faith in us, and so perfect is my love for you that I am, as it were, still, silent to my very soul.

I want nobody but you for my lover and my friend and to nobody but you shall I be faithful.

I am yours forever.

Tig.

Old love letters are best remembered

90

Love Letters in Richard Lovelace's Poetry

Richard Lovelace was an English poet of the seventeenth century. He expressed his love not in prose, but in poetry. The below poem is one of his best known works.

Here is a quote from another famous poem of his, 'To Lucasta, Going to the Wars':

> I could not love thee (Dear) so much,
> Lov'd I not Honour more.

To Althea, from Prison

> When Love with unconfinèd wings
> Hovers within my Gates,
> And my divine Althea brings
> To whisper at the Grates;
> When I lie tangled in her hair,
> And fettered to her eye,
> The Gods that wanton in the Air,
> Know no such Liberty.

When flowing Cups run swiftly round
With no allaying Thames,
Our careless heads with Roses bound,
Our hearts with Loyal Flames;
When thirsty grief in Wine we steep,
When Healths and draughts go free,
Fishes that tipple in the Deep
Know no such Liberty.

When (like committed linnets) I
With shriller throat shall sing
The sweetness, Mercy, Majesty,
And glories of my King;
When I shall voice aloud how good
He is, how Great should be,
Enlargèd Winds, that curl the Flood,
Know no such Liberty.

Stone Walls do not a Prison make,
Nor Iron bars a Cage;
Minds innocent and quiet take
That for an Hermitage.
If I have freedom in my Love,
And in my soul am free,
Angels alone that soar above,
Enjoy such Liberty.

Old love letters are best remembered

91

Subhas Chandra Bose to Emilie Schenkl

Subhas Chandra Bose, popularly known as Netaji, was one of the most famous freedom fighters of India who played a dynamic role in India's independence struggle. Born in Cuttack, Orissa, he also established the 'Hind Fauj.' His romance with the Austrian Emilie Schenkl was like a love story, with both keeping in touch through letters whenever they were apart.

(5 March 1936)

My darling, just as the snowy mountain melts when the time comes, so are my feelings. ...I don't know what will happen in the future... I may have to spend the rest of my life in jail. I should be shot or hanged. I will never be able to see you, but believe me, you will always rule in my heart. Will be in my thoughts and my dreams. If we could not meet in this life, I will be with you in the next life.

(1937)

...I just want to tell you that I am still as I was before. Not a single day has passed when I didn't think of you. You always be mine. I can't even think of anyone else. How sad I have been in these months, I felt lonely. Only one thing can keep me happy, but I don't know if it will be possible.

Old love letters are best remembered

Rupert Brooke to Noël Olivier

Rupert Brooke was an English poet famous for his idealistic war sonnets that he wrote during World War I, shortly before his death. He romanticized war. He was popular for his boyish good looks. It is believed that the Irish poet W.B. Yeats regarded him as 'the handsomest young man in England.'
In his poem 'The Soldier,' he wrote:

> *If I should die, think only this of me:*
> *That there's some corner of a foreign field*
> *That is forever towards England.*

He also wrote about love:

> *A kiss makes the heart young again and wipes out all the years.*

(2 October 1911)

[...]
   I have a thousand images of you in an hour; all different and all coming back to the same. [...] And we love. And we've got the most amazing secrets and understandings. Noel, whom I love, who is so beautiful and wonderful. I think of

you eating omelette on the ground. I think of you once against a sky line: and on the hill that Sunday morning.

And that night was wonderfullest of all. The light and the shadow and quietness and the rain and the wood. And you. You are so beautiful and wonderful that I daren't write to you… And kinder than God.

Your arms and lips and hair and shoulders and voice— you.

[…]

Old love letters are best remembered

93

Margery Paston to John Paston

Given below are two missives that have been taken from the Paston Letters, *a collection of letters written by various members of a Norfolk family of courtiers and scholars, which are considered a rich source of information regarding life in Medieval England. Both the letters have been written by Margery Paston, née Brews: the first when she was engaged to John Paston, and the second after they got married.*

(c. 1476–7)

Unto my Right Well Beloved Valentine, John Paston, Esquire
Be this Bill delivered

Right reverend and worshipful and my right well beloved valentine. I recommend me unto you full heartily, desiring to hear of your welfare, which I beseech Almighty God long for to preserve unto His pleasure and your heart's desire. And if it please you to hear of my welfare, I am not in good hele of body nor of heart, nor shall be till I hear from you:

> For there wots no creature what pain that I endure
> And for to be dead I dare it not discure (discover).

And my lady my mother hath laboured the matter to my father full diligently, but she can no more get than ye know of; for the which God knoweth I am full sorry. But if that ye love me, as I trust verily that ye do, ye will not leave me therefor. For if that ye had not half the livelihood that ye have, for to do the greatest labour that any Woman alive might I would not forsake you:

> And if ye command me to keep me true wherever I go
> I wins I will do all my might you to love and never no mo
> And if my friends say that I do amiss
> They shall not let (prevent) so for to do.
> Mine heart me bids ever more to love you
> Truly over all earthly things
> And if they be never so wroth
> I trust it shall be better in time coming.

No more to you at this time, but the Holy Trinity have you in keeping. And I beseech you that this bill be not seen of none earthly creature save only yourself.

And this letter was indited at Topcroft, with full heavy heart

By your own
MARGERY BREWS.

(21 January 1486)

Margery Paston to my Master, John Paston

Right reverend and worshipful sire. In my most humble wise

I recommend me to you, desiring to hear of your welfare, the which I beseech God to preserve to His pleasure, and so your heart's desire. Sir, I thank you for the venison that ye sent me; and your ship is sailed out of the haven as this day.

Sir, I send you by my brother William your stomacher of damask, As for your tippet of velvet, it is not here; Ann saith that ye put it in your casket at London.

Sir, your children be in good health, blessed be God. Sir, I pray you send me the gold that I spake to you of, by the next man that cometh to Norwich.

Sir, your mast that lay at Yarmouth is let to a ship of Hull for 13s. 4d., and if there fall any hurt thereto ye shall have a new mast therefore.

No more to you at this time, but Almighty God have you in His keeping. Written at Caistor, the 21st clay of January in the first year of King Henry VII, (1486).

By your servant,
MARGERY PASTON.
I pray God no ladies no more overcome you, that ye give no longer respite in your matters.

Old love letters are best remembered

94

David Hume to Madame de Boufflers

Born in 1711, David Hume was a Scottish philosopher, historian and economist. David Hume first met Madame de Boufflers when he was staying in Paris from 1763 to 1765. Although she was the mistress of Prince de Conti, Hume, in a mid-life crisis of sorts, developed an attachment to her. She, being much more well-versed than him in the ways of flirtation, gave Hume confusing signals, but it ultimately became clear to him that she wanted to marry the prince after her husband's death. He had no choice but to accept his fate, becoming her confidant instead of her lover.

(3 April 1766)

It is impossible for me dear madame, to express the difficulty which I have to bear your absence, and the continual want which i feel of your society. I had accustomed myself, of a long time, to think of you as a friend from whom I was never to be separated during any considerable time; and I had flattered myself that we were fitted to pass our lives in intimacy and cordiality with each other. Age and natural equality of temper were in danger of reducing my heart to too great indifference about everything, it was enlivened by the charms of your conversation, and the vivacity of your character. Your mind more agitated both by unhappy circumstances in your situation and by your natural disposition, could repose itself in the more calm sympathy which you found with me.

But behold! 3 months are elapsed since I left you; and it is impossible for me to assign a time when I can hope to join you. I still return to my wish, that I never left Paris, and that I had kept out of the reach of all other duties, except that which was so sweet, and agreeable, to fulfil, the cultivating your friendship and enjoying your society. Your obliging expressions revive this regret in the strongest degree; especially where you mention the wounds which, though skinned over, still fester at the bottom.

OH! my dear friend, how I dread that it may still be long ere you reach a state of tranquility, in a distress which so little admits of any remedy, and which the natural elevation of your character, instead of putting you above it, makes you feel with great sensibility. I could only wish to administer the temporary consolation, which the presence of a friend never fails to afford...

[...]

...I kiss your hands with all the devotion possible.
Hume.

Old love letters are best remembered

Count Gabriel Honoré de Mirabeau to Marie Thérèse de Monnier (Sophie)

Honoré-Gabriel Riqueti, comte de Mirabeau was a famous and controversial figure of the French Revolution. He is known for his scandalous love affairs, especially the one with Sophie, popularized by the letters the two exchanged.

(c. 1780)

Sophie,

To be with the people one loves, says La Bruyere is enough—to dream you are speaking to them, not speaking to them, thinking of them, thinking of the most indifferent things, but by their side, nothing else matters. O mon amie, how true that is! and it is also true that when one acquires such a habit, it becomes a necessary part of one's existence.

Alas! I well know, I should know too well, since the three months that I sigh, far away from thee, that I possess thee no more, than my happiness has departed. However, when every morning I wake up, I look for you, it seems to me that half of myself is missing, and that is too true.

Twenty times during the day, I ask myself where you are;

judge how strong the illusion is, and how cruel it is to see it vanish. When I go to bed, I do not fail to make room for you; I push myself quite close to the wall and leave a great empty space in my small bed. This movement is mechanical, these thoughts are involuntary. Ah! how one accustoms oneself to happiness.

Alas! one only knows it well when one has lost it, and I'm sure we have only learnt to appreciate how necessary we are to each other, since the thunderbolt has parted us. The source of our tears has not dried up, dear Sophie; we cannot become healed; we have enough in our hearts to love always, and, because of that, enough to weep always.

[...]

Gabriel

Old love letters are best remembered

96

Robert Peary to Josephine Peary

Robert Peary (1856–1920) was an American Arctic explorer born in Cresson, Pennsylvania, who led an expedition in 1909 that claimed to be the first to reach the North Pole. Peary's claim, though initially viewed with scepticism, and contested by rival Dr Frederick Cook, eventually gained widespread acceptance. He got married to Josephine Diebitsch on 11 August 1888. They spent most of the first 20 years of their marriage living apart from each other, with Josephine anxiously waiting while her husband fulfilled his ambitions of Arctic exploration.

(SS *Roosevelt*, 17 August 1908)

My Darling Josephine: Am nearly through with my writing. Am brain weary with the thousand and one imperative details and things to think of. Everything thus far has gone well, too well I am afraid, and I am (solely on general principles) somewhat suspicious of the future. The ship is in better shape than before; the party and crew are apparently harmonious; I have 21 Eskimo men (against 23 last time) but the total of men women and children is only 50 as against 67 before owing to a more careful selection as to children… I have landed supplies here, and leave two men ostensibly on behalf of Cook.

As a matter of fact I have established here the sub-base which last I established at Victoria Head, as a precaution in event of loss of the Roosevelt either going up this fall or coming down next summer. In some respects this is an advantage as on leaving here there is nothing to delay me or keep me from taking either side of the Channel going up. the conditions give me entire control of the situation...

You have been with me constantly, sweetheart. At Kangerdlooksoah I looked repeatedly at Ptarmigan Island and thought of the time we camped there. At Nuuatoksoah I landed where we were. And on the 11th we passed the mouth of Bowdoin Bay in brilliant weather, and as long as I could I kept my eyes on Anniversary Lodge. We have been great chums dear. Tell Marie to remember what I told her, tell 'Mister Man' [Robert Peary, Jr] to remember 'straight and strong and clean and honest', obey orders, and never forget that Daddy put 'Mut' in his charge till he himself comes back to take her. In fancy I kiss your dear eyes and lips and cheeks sweetheart; and dream of you and my children, and my home till I come again. Kiss my babies for me. Aufwiedersehen.

Love, Love, Love. Your Bert

P.S. August 18, 9 a.m. ...Tell Marie that her fir pillow perfumes me to sleep.

Old love letters are best remembered

Julia Lee-Booker to Lieutenant Pat McSwiney

Love requires sacrifices. Sometimes, it asks one to give up more than one ever thought possible, and all one can do is hope that in the end, the pain is worth the memories. This letter by Julia Lee-Booker evokes one such long-gone memory, the heart wishing it could freeze such moments in time.

(24 July 1940)

I cannot get that beautiful afternoon out of my head, above me where I lay the grass was silhouetted against the blue of the heavens, small clouds were rushing past as the wind drove them on an endless journey. Then close to me was the most lovely of all, your soft hair against my cheek, your kisses so cool and unearthly and my happiness was so great.

Old love letters are best remembered

Virginia Woolf to Vita Sackville-West

Virginia Woolf, born on 25 January 1882, was an English writer and one of the most prominent figures of the modernist literary movement. She first met Vita Sackville-West at a dinner party in 1922, and the meeting sparked a lifelong and passionate correspondence between the two writers. It is believed that Sackville-West was the inspiration behind Woolf's novel Orlando; Sackville-West's son went on to call the novel 'the longest and most charming love letter in literature.'

(1927)

Look here Vita—throw over your man, and we'll go to Hampton Court and dine on the river together and walk in the garden in the moonlight and come home late and have a bottle of wine and get tipsy, and I'll tell you all the things I have in my head, millions, myriads—They won't stir by day, only by dark on the river. Think of that. Throw over your man, I say, and come.

Old love letters are best remembered

Karl Marx to Jenny Von Westphalen

Karl Marx is better known as a German philosopher and was one of the most influential men who ever lived in the world. He was multi-faceted: a philosopher, economist, historian, socialist, political theorist, journalist, critic of political economy and socialist revolutionary. He wrote The Communist Manifesto *in 1848 and four volumes of* Das Kapital.

'If you love without evoking love in return—if through the vital expression of yourself as a loving person you fail to become a loved person, then your love is impotent, it is a misfortune,' he once stated.

As one who propagated the communist cause, he wrote: 'The communists have no need to introduce free love; it has existed almost from time immemorial.'

(Manchester, June 21, 1865)

My heart's beloved:

I am writing you again, because I am alone and because it troubles me always to have a dialogue with you in my head, without your knowing anything about it or hearing it or being able to answer.

[...]

Momentary absence is good, for in constant presence things seem too much alike to be differentiated. Proximity dwarfs even towers, while the petty and the commonplace, at close view, grow too big. Small habits, which may physically irritate and take on emotional form, disappear when the immediate object is removed from the eye. Great passions, which through proximity assume the form of petty routine, grow and again take on their natural dimension on account of the magic of distance. So it is with my love. You have only to be snatched away from me even in a mere dream, and I know immediately that the time has only served, as do sun and rain for plants, for growth.

The moment you are absent, my love for you shows itself to be what it is, a giant, in which are crowded together all the energy of my spirit and all the character of my heart. It makes me feel like a man again, because I feel a great passion; and the multifariousness, in which study and modern education entangle us, and the skepticism which necessarily makes us find fault with all subjective and objective impressions, all of these are entirely designed to make us all small and weak and whining. But love—not love for the Feuerbach-type of man, not for the metabolism, not for the proletariat—but the love for the beloved and particularly for you, makes a man again a man.

[...]

There are many females in the world, and some among them are beautiful. But where could I find again a face, whose every feature, even every wrinkle, is a reminder of the greatest and sweetest memories of my life? Even my endless pains, my irreplaceable losses I read in your sweet countenance, and I kiss away the pain when I kiss your sweet face.

[...]
Good-bye, my sweet heart. I kiss you and the children many thousand times.

Yours, Karl

Old love letters are best remembered

100

Fyodor Dostoevsky to Anna Dostoevskaya

Fyodor Dostoevsky was a renowned Russian short story writer, novelist, essayist and journalist. His literary works explore the human condition in the troubled times of nineteenth-century Russia. His most acclaimed novels include Crime and Punishment *(1866) and* The Idiot *(1869). Many consider him the greatest novelist in all of world literature.*

He once wrote: 'To love someone means to see them as God intended them.' Also: 'When there is love, you can live even without happiness.' However, paradoxically he wrote: 'But to fall in love does not mean to love.'

Significantly, Dostoevsky is often regarded as the ultimate heir to both European and Russian romanticism. His thesis statement on love was straight and simple: 'To love means in general to be good.'

My angel, you wrote me a sweet note that you often dream of me, etc. And I daydream about you. While drinking my coffee or tea I only think about you, not only about that thing alone, but in all senses. And so I'm convinced, Anya, that I not only love you, but also am in love with you and that you are my only mistress, and this is after 12 years! Yes, this is true, despite the fact that, of course, you have changed and aged since the time we first met. But now, believe me, I like you incomparably more. It would be incredible, but it's true. True, you are only 32 years old, and this is the blossoming period for a woman. I kiss you every minute in my dreams all the way, every minute passionately. I especially love that object about which it is said: 'And he is delighted with this charming object.' I kiss this object every minute in all ways and intend to kiss it all my life. Anechka, my dear, I can never, under any circumstances, leave you alone, my delightful naughty girl, because it's not only about naughtiness itself, but also that readiness, that charm and that intimacy of frankness with which I receive this naughtiness from you. Goodbye, I hug and kiss you passionately.

Old love letters are best remembered